# OLLA-PISKA
## *Tales of David Douglas*

WINNER

*Jasper G. and Minnie Stevens*
*Literary Prize*

2005

*In memory of Bonnie Hall,
whose art celebrates the wildflowers
of the Pacific Northwest*

# OLLA-PISKA

*Tales of David Douglas*

by Margaret J. Anderson

Oregon Historical Society Press
*Portland*

A JASPER G. & MINNIE STEVENS LITERARY PRIZE BOOK
Endowed in 2002 by Glen Kern Duffie to encourage authors to write
historical literature about Oregon. Mrs. Duffie, a long-time member of
the Oregon Historical Society, died in 2003.

*Visit our website at www.ohs.org.*

Printed in the United States of America

Distributed by the University of Washington Press

COVER ART AND DESIGN: Ellen Beier

INTERIOR ARTWORK: Watercolor paintings of plants by Bonnie Hall,
reprinted by permission of James D. Hall.

PRINTER: Thomson-Shore, Dexter, Michigan

*Library of Congress Cataloging-in-Publication Data*

Anderson, Margaret Jean, 1931–
Olla-Piska: tales of David Douglas / Margaret J. Anderson.
p. cm.
"A Jasper G. & Minnie Stevens Literary Prize Book."
Summary: Tells the story of botanist and explorer David Douglas's travels through the
Pacific Northwest in 1825–1827, from the point of view of a young apprentice.
Includes bibliographical references.
ISBN-13: 978-0-87595-297-0 (alk. paper)
ISBN-10: 0-87595-297-6 (alk. paper)
1. Douglas, David, 1799–1834—Juvenile fiction. [1. Douglas, David, 1799–1834—Fiction.
2. Botany—Fiction. 3. Northwest, Pacific—History—19th century—Fiction.]
I. Title. II. Title: Tales of David Douglas.
PZ7.A54397Oll 2006
[Fic]--dc22                                       2005037434

∞ The paper in this publication meets the minimum requirements of the
American National Standard for Information Sciences—Permanence of Paper for
Printed Library Materials, ANSI Z39.48-192.

# THE TALES

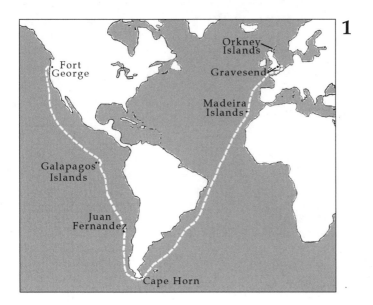

1

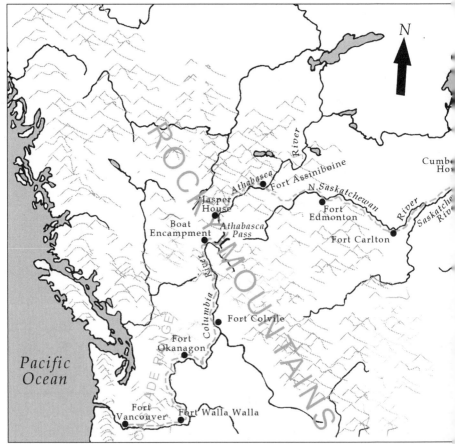

# The Travels of David Douglas

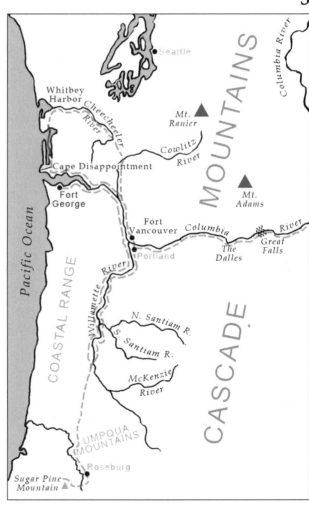

*Iris douglasiana* (Douglas iris)

# *Lessons from a Naturalist*

## by Sandy Ross
Cabin Boy on the *William and Ann*

*It is only when the wind blows furiously and the ocean is covered with foam like a washing-tub that I could take the Albatross. . . . He was very ferocious and would bite at sticks held out to him; one of the sailors in assisting me to lay hold of him was bitten in the thigh through the trousers — the piece was taken out as if cut with a knife.*

David Douglas' Journal,
Saturday, November 5, 1824

*"God save thee, ancient Mariner!*
*From the fiends, that plague thee thus! —*
*Why look'st thou so?" — With my cross-bow*
*I shot the Albatross.*

From "The Rime of the Ancient
Mariner," by Samuel Taylor
Coleridge, 1798

# CHAPTER 1

*Rousay, The Orkney Islands*
*January 1824*

My travels with David Douglas had their beginnings on a stormy day in January 1824 — though I didn't know it at the time. When I first wakened that morning, I could tell from a red-streaked patch of sky showing through the back window that I'd overslept. I could almost hear my father complaining about the big seaweed tangle that got away because I hadn't been there to help him bring it in.

Thinking there might still be time to make it to the beach before he came home, I grabbed my trousers, pulled them on, and then reached for my thick jersey, pushing my arms into sleeves that didn't quite cover my knobby wrists. Crossing the room in two strides, I quickly stirred the fire back to life. Next, I hung the porridge pot on its hook above the glowing peat.

As I left the house, I snatched John's coat from its peg by the back door. I still called the herringbone tweed jacket "John's coat," although it had been mine for over a year — ever since my twelfth birthday. John had already left home by then. He and Angus had signed on with the Hudson's Bay Company a year earlier.

Even though I knew my brothers were pledged to stay with the Company for five years, I kept hoping they would suddenly show up at the door, bragging about the bears they'd shot in those faraway forests. And the beavers they'd skinned. I'd never seen a bear or a beaver — or a forest for that matter. I hadn't even seen a tree! That seems strange now that they've played such a big part in my life.

When I stepped outside, I noticed the wind had dropped, but the storm waves were still pounding the shore. As I raced along the twisty path through the high dunes, I thought I heard voices. Maybe a quarrel had broken out over whose bit of shore a tangle of seaweed had washed up on. That happened a lot among us kelper families. We each guarded our own stretch of beach in the winter months.

When I reached the place where the path dropped off to the beach, I skidded to a stop. The red sky cast a warm glow on the sand below. But what were all those people doing down there so early in the day? They were bent over, knotted together in a tight crowd, carrying something heavy. As I jumped down to the beach in a hail of sand and pebbles, a woman broke away from the group and came running toward me—Aunt Agnes, with her shawl flapping and her bonnet askew.

"Sandy, lad! Sandy!" she called out. "Wait, wait! Stay where you are! It's Dougal, your father. They're taking him up to the house. Oh, laddie, laddie, my puir bairn, my puir orphan bairn!" She enveloped me in her shawl and rocked me against her as if I were a small child and not a lanky youth half a head taller than she was.

I tried to tell her to hold her talk, but the words kept pouring out. Words I didn't want to hear. It couldn't be true that the sea had taken my father. Dougal Ross was a strong man, tall and sure-footed. He was the bravest of all the kelpers. Everyone knew that. He would wade thigh-deep into the breaking waves and grapple a tumbling mass of weed with his pick. Then he'd drag the seaweed up to his section of the beach. He wasn't one of those men who let the tangles wash up wherever they willed and never set foot in the waves.

"I've been fearful for Dougal ever since we lost your dear mother," Aunt Agnes sobbed. "He wasn't the same after that. . . . I swear, he courted danger. . . . He should not have been out there in the surf on his own."

The time from that morning, when my father's lifeless body was carried up from the shore, to the evening, when he was laid in his final resting place in the little cemetery above the drying green, passed in a blur. After the funeral, Aunt Agnes took me back to her cottage facing the bay and told me I was welcome to stay as long as I wanted. I paid no heed to the mourners, who filled the house from morning till night, saying the same things over and over: *Poor, lonely lad, losing both his mother and father within a year . . . and his only brothers half a world away. How good of Agnes and Callum to take him in when they have five bairns of their own to provide for!*

I shared a bed with Ronnie and Alec, two of my young cousins. They were as silent as their mother was talkative. Ronnie, the older one, sometimes stared at me with solemn, dark eyes and touched my hand. He was seven, though in some ways he seemed younger. He'd been born with a clubfoot. He didn't spend as much time outdoors as the others, so he hadn't been toughened by their wild play.

As the weeks passed, anger gradually replaced the numbing sadness that seemed to fill my soul. I was angry with Aunt Agnes for going on about how my father had deliberately courted danger. That morning when they found him, she'd even gone so far as to wonder if he'd taken his own life, but Uncle Callum had hushed her. "Quiet, woman! If the minister hears you saying things like that, he'll refuse Dougal a Christian burial. Do you want your own brother to lie in unhallowed ground from now until eternity?"

But my rage was not all spent on Aunt Agnes. I was angry with my father as well. He should have been more careful. How were Angus and John going to feel when they came back and found that they had no home waiting for them? The laird had been quick to give the cottage and our kelp share to another tenant. There was no question of me taking over—I was too young. If Angus had only been there, he'd have been old enough. He was a man now, twenty years old.

I never went down to the beach anymore, and no one forced me. I mostly sat indoors, huddled over the peat fire. I was angry at the sea for taking my father's life. I was angry with the black-coated minister for saying that although it was beyond our understanding, it must be part of God's plan. I was angry with God.

Aunt Agnes urged the others to give me time. She said I'd get over my loss when the burning season came around. Then, during the long days of May and June, we would burn the brittle tangles of kelp on the drying green, just as we did each year, turning the dry weed to ash. The laird would then sell the ash to a factory in England, where they made iodine.

But I wasn't going to be there when it was time for burning. I had no idea *where* I might be.

As it turned out, young Ronnie would play an important part in my future, although we didn't guess it at the time. Because of his clubfoot, Ronnie was treated differently from the other McCallum children. He was the only one who attended the island school. Uncle Callum thought that being able to read and write might stand the boy in good stead, though there was not much call for book learning on Rousay — or on any of the Orkney Islands.

My uncle saw no need for his other children to go to school. Neither had my father, even though I'd have gone willingly enough if I'd been given the chance. I thought there was something magical about turning words into writing. I used to watch wee Ronnie as he sat cross-legged on the flagstone floor, carefully forming letters on his slate.

"What does it say?" I asked him one evening.

"This is my name across the top," he answered, running his finger along the top line of writing. "That's how you write *Ronald McCallum.*"

"Can you do *my* name?" I asked.

Ronnie quickly wrote two words under his own name. "I could get you your own slate and show you how to do it yourself," he offered. "There are some bits and pieces of slate on the green by the big house. They blew off the roof last winter."

Ronnie came home with the promised slate the next day. He had written *Alexander Ross* in big letters that took up most of the room. "I wrote Alexander instead of Sandy," he explained. "That's what the master would call you at school. He calls everyone by their real name. I'm always *Ronald* in school."

I studied my name for a while. I liked the look of the letters on the slate. "X" was a good plain letter. It would be easy to write. I traced the letters over with my finger until I could see the shape of my name with my eyes closed. Then I wiped the slate clean and tried to write it again. But my writing sprawled and went uphill, and I ran out of slate before I'd run out of the letters I needed to write. I cleaned off the slate and handed it to Ronnie, asking him to write *Alexander Ross* again. After a few more tries I could do it, and I kept at it until my writing was as small and tidy as Ronnie's. It felt good to be able to write my name.

With the coming of spring, I left the house more often, but I still didn't go up to the drying green to help Uncle Callum get the kelp ready for burning. Instead, every chance I got, I took the rowboat over to the big island we called Mainland. There, I met up with a crowd of older boys, who spent all their time talking about how to get away from the Orkney Islands. This was the kind of talk I thirsted for.

"Too bad the Hudson's Bay ships don't call in at Stromness any more. That used to be the best way out of here!"

"My brothers John and Angus signed up on the last ship," I volunteered. "I'm thinking of joining the Bay myself and going to look for them."

"The Bay'd never take you. You're too young."

"John was just sixteen, and I'm close to fourteen and tall for my age," I argued.

"If you're really set on the Hudson's Bay, Alisdair Clouston and Larry Flett are the people to talk to," someone suggested. "They're taking a fishing boat to Aberdeen next week and plan to sail from there to London. The Company signs people on all the time in London. But you'd need money to pay your way south."

"I have the money!" I said. Before I moved out of our cottage, I'd taken the money from the jar on the mantle — the money from last year's kelp harvest. I reckoned it was rightfully mine. Aunt Agnes had asked about it, but I couldn't see handing it over till I knew my own future.

Larry Flett was well known over on Rousay. He was a great fiddler and sometimes played at our *ceilidhs* when we brought in the New Year. Both he and Alisdair were fishermen's sons. Neither one of them was exactly encouraging when I said

I wanted to go along with them to London. But they weren't discouraging, either. I don't think they believed I could come up with the fare. Or maybe they didn't think I had the courage to follow through.

The only person on Rousay who I let in on my plan was wee Ronnie, and I swore him to secrecy.

"Cross your throat and hope to die if you tell anyone that I'm off to find John and Angus," I told him solemnly. "No matter how often people ask, you're not to say a word—not to a single soul. Not till I've been gone so long that there'll be no fetching me back."

Ronnie swore solemnly. Being a quiet lad, I figured I could count on him not to tell anyone. At least, not right away.

When I showed up on the pier on the appointed day, with the collar of John's jacket turned up against the wind and my father's old cap pulled down over my ears, Larry just said, "Let's go, lad!"

The tide was out, and the Aberdeen ship was riding low in the water. I had tied my few spare clothes in a blanket. Climbing down the metal ladder after Larry, I held the rail with one hand and my bundle in the other. When I reached the level of the deck, I jumped and landed on my backside, slithering across the wet deck.

"Welcome aboard!" Alisdair said, laughing as he pulled me to my feet.

As the ship pulled out, I stood by the rail, my thoughts completely taken up with the foolish start I'd made with Larry and Alisdair watching. But I had no room for any other regrets, as the Orkney Islands were swallowed up by the mist.

# CHAPTER 2

*Gravesend*
*July 1824*

We had a three-day wait for a southbound ship in Aberdeen, but I have no memory of that bustling harbor town. Or of the journey south following along the east coast of Scotland and England. I must have seen many fascinating things—my first trees and more kinds of people than I ever imagined—but they have all been blotted out by bigger trees and stranger people.

When we reached the mouth of the River Thames on the evening of Saturday, July 26, the Captain told us that there was no sense in going all the way to London. We'd do better getting off the ship at Gravesend. That's where ocean-going vessels docked, and it was the best place to look for a ship that was sailing to North America.

*Gravesend.* The name had an ominous ring to it. It didn't sound like a good place for the start of a voyage.

Darkness was falling when we docked, and shadowy figures lurked among the boxes of cargo. Gravesend didn't look like a good place for ending a voyage, either.

The Captain seemed to have the same thought.

"You lads should stay at the Cross Keys Inn tonight," he told us. "That way you can check out the ships in daylight. You want to be careful in these seaport towns. There's no saying where you might end up."

With the Captain's warning ringing in our ears, we weren't eager to leave our cramped attic room at the inn, but hunger finally drove us down to the bar. It was noisy and poorly lit, with more men packed in than you'd find on all of Rousay. At least, that's how it seemed to me. We huddled together in a dim corner, eating our bread and cheese and sipping mugs of ale, trying to make ourselves invisible. But we didn't succeed. We hadn't been there five minutes before a man dressed in sailor garb slid onto the bench across from us.

"What brings you lads here?" he asked.

"We're not planning on staying," Larry said quickly, as if the man was challenging us. "We're going to sign on with the Hudson's Bay Company. We want to go to Rupert's Land."

"If it's the Hudson's Bay you're after, you should talk to Three-fingered Jack!" The sailor stood up and looked about the room. Waving his arms wildly, he shouted, "Hey, Jack! Over here! I've got some new recruits."

We waited nervously as a short man pushed his way through the crowd. He had a rugged, weather-beaten face and long gray hair braided into a single pigtail. The hand that held his mug of ale was missing two fingers.

"Where do you lads hail from?" he asked, settling himself on the bench beside the sailor.

"The Orkney Islands," Alisdair answered.

"A barren place, I hear! The sort of place people want to leave behind, judging from the number of men from the Orkneys that I ran into when I worked for the Bay."

The mention of men from the Orkneys got my attention.

"Do you know my brothers—John and Angus Ross?" I asked boldly.

"Can't say I ever met them," he answered. "Maybe they got lost in the shuffle when the North West Company and the Hudson's Bay merged three years back. That's when George Simpson—he's Governor of the Northern Department—sent a lot of Scotsmen out to the Pacific side."

"The Pacific side?" Larry echoed.

"Where the mighty Columbia River runs into the ocean. That's where you should aim to go. They say it's a great new country, teeming with beaver just waiting to be trapped. And trees that reach the sky. The mountains gleam white with snow even in the summertime, and the river's as wide as the English

Channel, with more fish than you can imagine. You can cross the water walking on their backs."

Three-fingered Jack was like a preacher talking about the Promised Land. He held us spellbound. Here was a man who had really lived. He'd spent eight years in Rupert's Land, traveling through the country with Indians. He'd been lost in blizzards and stalked by wolves. He had wrestled with bears.

"Was it a bear that got your fingers?" I asked.

"Naw! That was a steel trap—snapped shut before I was ready, and two of my fingers went flying off. I stumbled back into camp, holding my hand above my head so I wouldn't bleed to death!"

I listened, wide-eyed.

"If you lads are really serious about signing on with the Hudson's Bay, you've struck gold! The *William and Ann* is leaving in a few days for the Columbia, and they still need extra hands."

The next morning, we spotted the *William and Ann* right away. Her three tall masts reached higher than those of any other ship in the harbor. She was a fine-looking brig, about four times as long as the twenty-foot boat that had brought us from Orkney. The deck was a flurry of activity, and one of the sailors confirmed what Three-fingered Jack had told us the night before. An outbreak of measles had left them short of men. We should talk to the recruiting officer, he said, pointing to one of the tumbledown buildings that ringed the harbor.

As we approached the shack, a man in a dark blue uniform came out to meet us. He was ready to sign on Alisdair and Larry as soon as he heard their Orkney voices. But when it came to me, he shook his head and told me to go back to my family. "We'll take you on when you have some meat on your bones," he said.

"I have no family," I answered, struggling to keep my voice low. It had this way of going squeaky when I least wanted it to. I cleared my throat and added, "My mother died a year ago, and my father drowned last winter. All I have is my brothers, John and Angus. They're with the Hudson's Bay Company."

"Do you know where they are?"

"They said in a letter a while back that George Simpson might send them out to the Columbia."

I hadn't set out to lie to the officer, but my head was so full of Three-fingered Jack's tales that I could clearly see John and Angus out there in the Columbia country, tracking wild animals through the never-ending forest.

What I couldn't picture was the letter I said my brothers had sent home. Neither of them knew how to write! And even if someone had written a letter for them, they'd have thought twice about sending it, since no one in our family could read.

"You must have some people back in Orkney," the officer insisted. "Aunts or uncles?"

"I can't go back. I spent all my money getting here," I answered.

That, at least, was the plain truth.

"So what will you do?"

"I'll get a job in London till I'm old enough to sign on," I answered, with a lot more bravado than I felt.

The officer stared at me for several minutes, while I tried to read my future in the smoke spiraling up from his pipe. "Come back later," he said, getting to his feet. "I'll have a word with Captain Hanwell and see if he'll take you on as a cabin boy. Once you're there, they'll likely be able to use you in the Company store. There's a lot of record-keeping and the like."

"Record-keeping?" I repeated.

"Writing down the number and the kinds of skins that the trappers bring in. And then there's the keeping track of the supplies."

Alisdair and Larry had taken off to look over the *William and Ann*, leaving me on my own. I felt totally abandoned.

What followed were just about the longest two hours of my life. I sat on an upturned barrel next to the office door, thinking about my future. If the Captain wouldn't have me, what could I do in London? The only thing I knew was how to wrestle kelp tangles from the sea and tend fires on the beach. I'd be better off going straight back to Orkney. But how could I do that with no money?

I didn't think I could work my passage. Alisdair and Larry knew about boats, being fishermen's sons. On the way down to Aberdeen, they'd swaggered around the deck, lending a hand with ropes and anchors, while I'd flopped about like a beached fish. All I could do was keep out of the way.

And suppose this Captain Hanwell did agree to have me. What was a cabin boy expected to do? I could picture the Captain growing angry at my landlubber ways and tossing me overboard. I couldn't even swim. And then there was this business of writing down the kinds of skins the trappers brought in.

So I didn't feel any joy when the officer came back and told me that he'd worked things out with the Captain. He handed me a sheet of paper, explaining that it was a letter of introduction to the head person. He called him the Chief Factor.

"Sign your name at the bottom of the page."

I looked at the paper, wishing I knew what all those words said. Then I carefully wrote *Alexander Ross* as neatly as I knew how. What a lucky thing that Ronnie had taught me to write my name! Maybe it was all meant to be after all. Maybe everything would fall into place. Maybe Angus and John would be there waiting for me when I reached the Columbia.

At least, I had somewhere to stay for the next nine months — for that's how long the officer said we'd be at sea.

Taking back the letter, the officer glanced at it and said, "Good luck to you, lad! You'll go a long way with that fine penmanship!" Then he folded the letter and sealed it shut with a blob of wax, impressed with the Company crest. When he handed it back to me, I thanked him and gave him a weak grin. I wasn't about to spoil the moment by telling him those were the only two words I knew how to write!

# CHAPTER 3

*The Madeira Islands*
*August 1824*

By the time the *William and Ann* set sail the following afternoon, I knew my way around the ship. Now that I was on board, it didn't seem so big. I'd been assigned a hammock belowdecks and a place to stow my bundle. Beyond that, no one paid me any heed. I was half-scared of being given a task I didn't know how to do, but at the same time I wanted to look busy.

We hadn't even reached the mouth of the river when the Captain gave the order to drop anchor. At this rate, it would be two days before we reached the open sea. Small wonder the voyage was going to take nine months!

The next morning, we were underway before daybreak. It was cold and foggy, the kind of morning I never liked on Rousay. The fog was so thick that we could not see the shore when we ran aground on the Shivering Sands. We sat there, helpless, for more than an hour, beaten about by the wind and waves until the incoming tide floated us free. Several inches of water had leaked into the hold, so Captain Hanwell announced that we'd have to stop in Portsmouth to await orders from the Company about what to do next.

Several of the sailors were uneasy, muttering that this was a bad start to the voyage. But when I said as much to Charlie Crabtree, the cook, he just shrugged and said this was how every voyage started out.

"It's never plain sailing! Why don't you peel some of those spuds, lad, and stop your worrying!"

That's how I became Charlie's helper in the cramped quarters of the galley, deep in the bowels of the ship. Huge pots and pans swung from the beams. By the flickering light of an oil lamp, I could see that a row of barrels that lined one wall were labeled with words I couldn't read. I was glad that Charlie had asked me to do something familiar. I knew how to boil potatoes, because I'd helped with the cooking after Ma died. But I'd never before been faced with the mound of spuds it took to feed thirty hungry men!

The Captain must have judged the ship to be seaworthy while we made our way along the south coast. He didn't put in at Portsmouth after all.

We left the rocky shores of Cornwall behind on the last day of July, and that's when I found out about seasickness. For a few days, I was no use to Charlie or anyone else, but then I got my sea legs — or, rather, my sea stomach.

The ranking on the ship was not so very different from the way things had been on Rousay. The crew and the Hudson's Bay men were like the fishermen, farmers, and kelpers back on the island — ordinary folk who did all the work, some more than others. Captain Hanwell was on top, like the laird. His cabin was all rich wood and gleaming brass.

The Captain had our fortunes in his hand. He could make our lives miserable or not. He could have a sailor whipped, but he could also order a round of grog. Sometimes, he even joined us on nights when we sang together on deck. My ranking was pretty much like it had been at home, where I was at everyone's beck and call. I was owned by no one, but that meant I had to answer to everyone — cleaning up messes, coiling miles of rope, polishing brasses, and especially doing Charlie's bidding in the galley. After I peeled the potatoes that first day, he seemed to think he had more claim on me than anyone else and would box my ears if, through no fault of my own, I showed up late to help.

Two gentlemen did not fit the pattern. They mostly kept themselves apart from the crew. Charlie sometimes had me take their meals to them in their cabin, which was quite big, but not as fancy as the Captain's. One of the men — John Scouler — was the ship's doctor. He also led prayers on Sunday mornings.

The other man was David Douglas. His place on the ship wasn't clear at all. He was Scottish—a slight man with reddish hair that was thinning even though he was only in his mid-twenties. He had instruments that told the temperature of the air and the sea. Even when the ship was surrounded by nothing but sky and water, he took note of where we were. He was a quiet man, and he was a great one for writing. He entrusted more words to his notebook than he did to the crew. Seeing him writing in his journal was a nagging reminder of what was waiting for me at the end of the voyage.

After we'd been at sea for ten days and I was well over being seasick, we reached the Madeira Islands, about three hundred and fifty miles from the northwest coast of Africa. Everyone was excited because we would be going ashore. I was more than ready to stand on firm land.

I thought I'd feel at home on Madeira because it was an island, but it turned out to be quite different from home. The biggest difference was the colors. On the Orkney Islands, the colors are soft. On Madeira, they are so vivid that you have to close your eyes to rest them. And the things that grow there! Banana trees with each leaf as big as a hammock. Charlie Crabtree took me to the vegetable market, and I helped him pick out two buckets of lemons. Then he handed me a banana and told me to eat it.

"Peel it first!" he said, laughing, when the banana was halfway to my mouth.

Even peeled, I didn't really care for the mushy taste, but I ate it anyway because Charlie acted as if he was offering me a great treat.

Before we went ashore, I'd made up my mind that this was going to be where I'd spend my last shillings. And I wasn't going to spend the money on food or drink, though the islands are famous for their grapes and wine. I'd overheard John Scouler and David Douglas say they were planning to buy enough Madeira wine to see them through the rest of the voyage.

But I had something more practical in mind. For the last few days, I'd been sweltering in my Orkney woolens. So I bought myself a bright yellow cotton shirt, a pair of tan sailcloth trousers, and rope sandals.

As soon as I was back on the ship, I put on my new clothes and scampered up the ladder to the middle deck, where Scouler and Douglas had their cabin. In case one of them was around, I had a couple of wine glasses I'd taken from the galley. I planned to say that Charlie Crabtree had suggested they'd be wanting them so they could sample their wine.

When no one answered my knock, I slipped inside the cabin and went over to the mirror. Any time I was in there, I stopped in front of that mirror. If I was alone, I'd run my fingers through my hair, pulling it up into horns. Then I'd squint my eyes and wrinkle my nose. I looked so funny that I had to laugh out loud. But this time, I drew myself up tall, so I could see the yellow shirt. I liked what I saw of myself — my thin, tanned face and blue eyes and sun-bleached hair. Father always said I had Viking blood.

As I turned to leave, I noticed David Douglas' hat lying on his bunk. I blinked and took a step closer to make sure my eyes weren't playing tricks on me. The hat was completely smothered in dead insects — beetles and grasshoppers and butterflies. They covered the entire brim and the crown. But the uncanny thing was that the insects had all been stabbed with pins. The pins held them in place.

Then I spotted two dead birds and a live snake in a jar. The bunk was strewn with wilting plants — leaves and flowers and seeds. They weren't like the bright bunches of wildflowers Ma used to pick to brighten up our cottage. They were more like the baskets of herbs and roots that old Granny Gaddes gathered — thyme and asphodel and sprigs of white heather. She was widely known for her love potions, but she dealt in other spells, too. There wasn't much use for love potions on the *William and Ann*. That left the other spells.

As I scooted down the ladder to the galley, I was thinking that from then on I'd give David Douglas a wide berth. I wasn't going to make any more faces in his mirror. Who knows but what my face might stay that way!

When the tanks had been filled with fresh water and all the baskets of fresh vegetables had been brought on board, the *William and Ann* was ready for the long haul across the Atlantic.

While Charlie and I were stowing away the last of the produce, he told me that this would be the longest stretch of water out of sight of land. "It takes us across the equator," he added with a cheerful grin.

"What's the equator?" I asked.

Charlie never was one to give a straight answer. All he would say was, "What did they teach you at school?"

I chased after a lemon that was rolling across the floor. I wasn't about to tell him I'd never been to school. I didn't want it known that I'd been signed on to keep records in the Company store when I didn't know how to read or write.

When we finally reached the equator, I discovered it wasn't something you could see. It was just a reason for a wild party. The Captain issued extra rations of grog, and those of us who were crossing the equator for the first time were tossed in a sail filled with water. David Douglas and I ended up being tossed in the same sail. I laughed almost as much at Douglas as at myself — the way he lost his properness!

The following day we saw flying fish, skipping from wave to wave. The fish in the waters around the Orkney Islands never take to the air. Because the *William and Ann* was low in the water, a number of them fluttered on board. Douglas was out there catching what he called *specimens*. The ones the rest of us caught ended up as fish stew. We called them *dinner*!

By this time, the bright sun and heavy rains had washed most of the color out of my new clothes, but I was no shabbier than anyone else — except, of course, the Captain and Doctor Scouler and David Douglas, who dressed like gentlemen. Some of the Hudson's Bay men had good clothes packed away, but on ship they dressed like sailors. I asked Larry and Alisdair if we'd be needing proper clothes, but they said that we could worry about that at the end of the journey.

It wasn't a dark worry — like not being able to read.

The day we were finally within sight of the coast of South America started out with high seas and heavy showers. By noon the sky had cleared and the wind had dropped. Then, at two o'clock, there came an excited cry from high in the rigging: "*Land ahead!*"

Soon flocks of birds and huge swarms of butterflies welcomed us to Brazil. David Douglas and John Scouler got in everyone's way, waving nets and taking aim at the poor birds. One of the sailors told me that this was because they were naturalists. I wanted to ask what a naturalist did with the dead things, but thinking that this was maybe something I should have learned at school, I held my tongue.

# CHAPTER 4

*Tierra del Fuego*
*December 1824*

We were now sailing down the east coast of South America, and I was tired of traveling. I was tired of the sameness. The same ocean, the same sky, the same birds circling the ship. Watching the birds, I wished myself back on Rousay — lying on the close-cropped drying greens with the other lads, watching the wheeling fulmar and the silver sheen of the gannet's wing.

Here on the ship, I was lonely, even though I was hardly ever alone. Alisdair and Larry had found mates among the crew, but I had no one. Maybe it was because I was younger than the others. Or maybe it was because Alisdair and Larry were good at everything — trimming sails and climbing the rigging — while I was all thumbs, especially when I was helping Charlie Crabtree in the galley. I now knew why the sailors called him Old Crab. He had a sharp tongue and took it out on me when things went wrong. When the sailors complained about the meat being off, he acted like it was my fault — even when I'd had no hand in the cooking.

One morning, while I was washing plates in the galley, I got to worrying about what was going to happen at the end of the journey. On Rousay, I could always figure a way out of a tight corner, but there was no way to pretend to be able to read and write. I'd heard enough times that the Hudson's Bay Company was strict on rules. If you didn't live by the rules, you ended up with your legs in irons.

I blinked away the sad picture of my skinny ankles rubbed raw by the irons just as Charlie tossed me a greasy lump of fat pork. "Take this up to David Douglas!" he ordered. "You'll find him on the upper deck with Bo'sun Black."

Douglas, who was usually polite, all but grabbed the raw meat out of my hand. I couldn't think what he was he going to do with it, and I wasn't about to go below until I found out. So I settled myself on a coil of rope and waited

For a bit, he and Black did nothing more than talk, standing there with their heads close together, Douglas still holding the pork. I finally gave up watching them and turned my attention to the albatross that had been following us for several days. It rode the wind effortlessly, flying so easily that it seemed to have no weight at all. Sailors like to see an albatross. They say the bird brings good luck—and we'd be needing lots of good luck. We'd soon be rounding Cape Horn, the graveyard of many a brave ship.

Suddenly, the Bo'sun marched off, saying he'd be back in a minute. He returned, carrying a large hook tied to a length of rope and several heavy sticks. It wasn't until Douglas baited the hook with the pork that I realized what the two men were about. They were going to try to catch the albatross! Their plan was to lure the bird down onto the deck with the lump of pork, where it would have a hard time taking off again. An albatross has to put a lot of effort into lifting its own weight. I'd seen one take off from the surface of the sea, raising itself up like an angry swan defending its nest, part running and part flying, the points of its wings skimming the waves and sending up a shower of spray until it slowly rose into the air.

I willed the bird to stay aloft, but hunger won out. It landed on the deck on splayed black feet and took a stab at the meat. When it tried to take off again, Douglas and the Bo'sun closed in on it, beating it with their sticks. The albatross put up a good fight. I almost cheered when it bit clear through Bo'sun Black's trousers taking a hunk of flesh, but then Douglas pinned it against the rail and stabbed it. Ignoring the blood and bile that stained the dead bird's gleaming feathers, he stretched out the black-tipped wings and measured them.

"Twelve feet and four inches," he said proudly. "An astonishing specimen!"

I didn't wait to see him take the battered bird down to his

cabin. I just hoped that the smell of its rotting flesh would make him sick.

That same night, the wind picked up. We were nearing the dreaded Cape. By dawn, we were tossing about on a frenzied sea. The slow climb to the top of each glassy wave was followed by the heart-stopping moment when the prow was suspended in space. Then the ship, which seemed to have shrunk in size, started the long slide down into the trough with the next wave looming higher than the one before. The noise was deafening, as timbers creaked and canvas snapped against the backdrop of the roaring winds. Down in the galley, pans and tin plates crashed about in a wild dance. Then came a frightening moment when the ship changed course and caught the waves side on.

"Is this the worst storm you've ever seen?" I asked Charlie breathlessly, clinging to the table. We were struggling to fix rations for the weary crew.

"We're in the lap of the gods right enough," Charlie answered quietly. "But I've come through worse."

As the days wore on, Captain Hanwell, grim-faced but calm, barked orders and the crew obeyed, even when doing his bidding put them in mortal danger. They lowered the mainsails so they wouldn't be torn from the mast while still trying to hold the ship on course. But Hanwell never gave the only order that I knew would save the ship. The *William and Ann* would never round the Cape with a dead albatross on board! Surely he knew that.

Ten days after Douglas killed the albatross, I decided to take matters into my own hands. If no one else was going to do anything, then it was up to me. I cautiously made my way toward his cabin. A few minutes earlier, I'd heard him talking with the doctor on the upper deck. I had no idea how I was going to get the giant bird up the ladder and onto the deck without being stopped, but the first step was to get hold of it.

I never did accomplish that first step. When I opened the cabin door, I found myself face to face with David Douglas. Doctor Scouler must have been talking to someone else.

"What can I do for you, lad?" he asked.

" I . . . I want to save us from the storm," I stammered, too shaken to come up with anything else.

"To save us from the storm?"

"I . . . I was going to throw the albatross into the sea. Killing it has brought bad luck."

"Throwing it into the sea won't bring it back to life," Douglas answered. "Nor will it change anyone's luck — or quiet the winds, either. Only God can do that. The storms off the Cape test every ship that passes this way. In truth, we didn't fare as badly as most, and the worst is already behind us."

Now that I thought about it, we did seem to be riding the waves more easily. At the height of the storm, we couldn't have heard one another's voices above the noise. But that didn't change the fact that the albatross was dead.

"You shouldn't have killed it," I said sullenly. "We'll all pay for it before the journey's end."

"If anyone pays, it should be me," Douglas answered. "And I wouldn't be the first collector to fail to reach home with my treasures. I only pray that I'm rewarded with some small measure of success."

"Treasures?" I echoed, fixing on the one word that meant anything to me.

"Aye, the treasures of nature," Douglas explained. "I search out specimens of plants and animals that aren't found in England. Birds like the albatross. Its skin will go back with the ship and end up in a museum in London, stuffed and mounted, for people to look at."

The word *museum* was new to me, but I did know that a dead bird was nothing like a living one. I could see why the Hudson's Bay trappers would go after beaver so that the rich folk in England could have their fur collars and top hats, but to send a dead bird back to London for people just to look at made no sense at all.

Then I had another thought. "All those beetles and flies and dead flowers — are they for this museum?" I asked.

"Some of the beetles will end up in glass boxes in people's homes," Douglas said. "The flowers and shrubs are for their gardens. The people back home are eager to have plants from faraway places."

"The laird once tried to plant trees on Rousay, but they didn't grow. Flowers and trees are better off blooming where they belong."

"Plants are a bit like people, Sandy," Douglas answered. "Some flourish in foreign places, and some never put down roots. It's mostly seeds I'll be taking back, though I need to press the flowers and leaves, too, so that we can give the plants their right Latin names."

After that, I tried to keep out of Douglas' way, but now he seemed to be everywhere. One morning I was truly cornered. I was leaning over the rail, holding a stout rope tied to a side of beef that was bouncing over the surface of the water, leaving a frothy wake behind it. Charlie had sent me up on deck to wash the coating of salt and green slime from the meat. When it was clean, we'd hack it into chunks and serve it up as a thick stew called lobscouse. The sailors complained that Charlie's lobscouse tasted like horsemeat flavored with rusty harnesses, but even so, they scraped their bowls clean. Hard work and fresh air sharpened all our appetites.

While I was washing the meat, I had my eye on the dark cone-shaped island of Mas-a-Fuero, which was falling away behind us. I hoped the Captain had been right when he decided against putting in there to take on fresh water. Charlie had told me that we were going to be in big trouble if we didn't reach Juan Fernandez before the casks were empty. It would be a shame to die of thirst, he said, while surrounded by nothing but water.

I'd just decided that the meat was clean enough and was dragging it in, when I became aware of an extra hand pulling on the rope. Turning around, I found myself face to face with David Douglas! A huge length of seaweed was caught up in the rope, and he wanted a closer look.

"Look at the size of that piece of kelp!" he exclaimed. "It must be more than thirty feet long."

The strong iodine smell of the seaweed filled me with a rush of homesickness, and I found myself confiding in him without meaning to.

"I've seen bigger pieces than this back on Rousay," I told him. "Me and my family used to collect the weed that washed up on the shore in the winter gales. It was hard and dangerous work raking in the tangles before the waves could snatch them back again."

"The tangles?"

"Aye, that's what we call the tumbling seaweed that comes in on the big waves. We would drag it up onto the banks out of reach of the sea and leave it there till spring. Then we spread it on the drying green till it was ready for burning."

"Do you miss your home?" Douglas asked me, turning over the wet kelp. He pounced on a small crablike creature that was clinging to its shiny brown surface.

My fingers were numb from the pull of the rope. I flexed them while I thought about his question.

"There's no place as beautiful in the summertime," I said. "That's when we burn the weed. In summer, we draw close to one another, forgetting the rivalries of the winter months. We laze around, singing and telling stories, while the little ones play. Every now and then, someone gets up to tend one of the smoldering fires, adding a few more tangles and watching that the flames don't burst free."

I found myself painting Douglas a word picture of the purple heather on the moors and the close-cropped fields, carpeted with buttercups and clover. Douglas told me that those flowers also have Latin names. He learned them when he was in the Highlands with his botany teacher, Professor Hooker.

"I loved the way the larks sang all day long and far into the evening," he said.

"Did you ever have a mother bird draw you away from her nest by faking a broken wing?" I asked. "You follow her, thinking this time you'll surely catch up with her, but when you're far enough from the nest, she takes off into the air and you see that there's nothing wrong with her wing after all!"

"I think you have the makings of a naturalist," Douglas said, smiling down at me.

I was about to ask him what he meant when he changed the subject. "I hear you're hoping to find your brothers in the Columbia country. And that you're going to be helping keep records in the store."

"Aye," I agreed cautiously.

"We'll be putting ashore on Juan Fernandez soon," Douglas said. "I expect to pick up a lot of plant specimens there. Would you like me to ask the Captain if he could spare you to do some record-keeping? You could help me write the labels."

"I . . . I don't think so," I stammered. "Charlie couldn't manage without me in the galley. And I . . . I have to get this meat back down there right now!"

# CHAPTER 5

*Juan Fernandez*
*December 1824*

All this time, I had, at the back of my mind, a picture of my brothers waiting for me by a wide river teeming with fish. We'd head off into the woods to trap beaver. When we came back with a huge pile of skins, the Chief Factor would realize that I was born to be a trapper. Keeping records would be a waste of my talents. But now, David Douglas was out to spoil everything. When he found out that I could neither read nor write, he'd tell the Captain, who would think that I'd lied to the recruiting officer. Captain Hanwell would probably cast me ashore the first chance he got.

Well, I wasn't going to wait for that to happen! I decided that I was going to make the first move. When we put ashore for water at Juan Fernandez, I would jump ship.

It wasn't such a crazy idea. Just a few days earlier, Charlie Crabtree had told me that Juan Fernandez was Robinson Crusoe's island. The name *Robinson Crusoe* meant nothing to me, but I was soon caught up in Charlie's story.

Crusoe was the lone survivor of a ship that wrecked off the shores of Juan Fernandez years and years ago. Somehow, he saved enough supplies from the sunken ship to live alone on the island for twenty-eight years — though, according to Charlie, he wasn't really alone. Two cats and a dog survived the wreck as well. And then there was someone called Man Friday. And the cannibals.

"Cannibals?" I repeated

"People who eat human flesh," Charlie explained.

The meat that I was chopping for the lobscouse suddenly looked even less inviting than usual.

Charlie said that a man called Daniel Defoe made up the story about Robinson Crusoe. But the next night, Doctor Scouler told us that the idea was based on a real person who lived on Juan Fernandez for four years before being rescued. His name was Alexander Selkirk. He was a Scottish shoemaker's son who ran away to sea when he was just a lad. While his brig was sailing along the west coast of South America, he dreamed that it was going to sink, so he asked the Captain to put him ashore on Juan Fernandez.

"And did it sink?" I asked.

"Yes! As a matter of fact, it did! When Selkirk was rescued, that was *his* first question. His saviors told him that the ship had foundered and every last man drowned. Alexander Selkirk came by his second sight honestly. He was the seventh son of a seventh son."

I liked that the real Robinson Crusoe's name had been Alexander. I also liked that he had stayed on the island for only four years. I was counting on a southbound ship putting in for water and rescuing me. I would explain to the captain that I had deserted the *William and Ann* because it had a curse on it after David Douglas killed an albatross. As the third son of a third son, I'd known that trouble was looming.

When we dropped anchor in Cumberland Bay on Juan Fernandez, I scarcely heard the wild cheers of the crew or the rattle of the anchor chain. My eyes were fixed on the island's rugged outline. The tops of the mountains were lost in the clouds, their lower slopes clothed in dark trees, much different from the green and gold hills of the Orkneys. But it didn't really matter what Juan Fernandez looked like from the sea. What mattered was what it was like when I went ashore. I'd need a cave for shelter and shellfish and coconuts to fend off hunger. And maybe a small dog for company.

I'd counted on Charlie giving me the job of filling the water casks the first day, but he wanted to do it himself because it gave him a reason to go ashore. So I took the rash step of asking David Douglas if I could help him collect the plants I was going to be labeling. I asked confidently, knowing that I wouldn't be there to write the labels. Douglas agreed with a friendly smile and said I could carry his vasculum—a battered tin box with a leather shoulder strap.

When the ship's boat was lowered, I was one of the first on board. I scrunched down between two empty flasks, trying to make myself as small as I could. Larry and Alisdair settled themselves in the bow with their fishing poles. They were supposed to bring back fish for our supper. I wondered if I could talk them out of a couple of hooks. I'd need some way to catch fish. I was also going to need some way to start a fire. Today's trip was just to get a feel for the land, but there was a lot to think about.

As the ship neared the shore, Doctor Scouler pointed out a small vessel at the far end of the bay. Then Bo'sun Black spotted a thin column of smoke rising from a hut nestled in the brush. The stone walls and straw roof reminded me of the farmhouses on Orkney, but this hut seemed more sinister somehow. Maybe it was the way plants climbed up over it, as if it was trying to hide.

At that moment a wild figure leapt out of the brush and came running toward the water's edge. He was flailing his arms about and seemed to want us to dock in a wooded creek at the east end of the bay. I wouldn't have trusted him, but Black ordered the oarsmen to bring the boat round. "Easy on the larboard side!" he shouted.

We headed for the dark inlet.

Several of the crew jumped into the shallow water and began to drag the boat up into the creek. I hung back, lining up the empty casks, but the wild man came splashing into the water and grabbed one of them, smothering us with a torrent of words. At first, I thought he was talking in a foreign tongue, but when he slowed down a bit I realized he was speaking English. He told us his name was William Clark and he was from London.

"How did you end up here?" someone asked.

"I came over from Chile with some Spaniards who've gone to the other side of the island to hunt seals and bullocks. The skins fetch a good price in Coquimbo. They left me here to keep an eye on the boat. When I saw your ship anchored in the bay, I took you for pirates, so I hid. Then I heard you speaking

English! You can't believe how good it is to hear English after all this time."

When the sailors turned their attention to filling the water casks, David Douglas asked Mister Clark to show Doctor Scouler and him around the island. He was only too happy to agree. Since I was carrying the vasculum, I trailed along after them. I was frantically trying to figure out how Clark and the Spaniards were going to fit in with my plan. Did I want to go back to Chile with them, or would I be better off waiting for another ship?

Clark led us up to the hut on the beach, ushering us in as proudly as if he was welcoming us to a manor house. But the hut offered no more inside than the outside promised. The room had a bed in the corner, just a bunch of straw and a ragged blanket. The only other furniture was a seaman's chest. Clark threw it open and showed us his library of books. Seventeen books in all, including the Bible, a Book of Common Prayer, and *Robinson Crusoe*. Doctor Scouler read off the names. The wild man was a scholar! I almost groaned. There was no getting away from books and reading, even here on a deserted island.

"You've got a copy of Cowper's poems!" Doctor Scouler said, pouncing on a small, square book with a leather cover. He took it outside so he could see the words.

"I know 'Alexander Selkirk' by heart," Clark said, following Doctor Scouler to the door. He threw out his arms and roared, "*I am monarch of all I survey. My right there is none to dispute. From the centre all round to the sea, I am lord of the fowl and the brute.*"

It dragged me down to discover that William Clark was a bookish man. When he finally put everything away, he offered to take us to see the remains of an old orchard.

"It's in a clearing up on the hillside," he said. "The Spaniards had a colony here years ago, but they abandoned it."

As we followed Clark up the hill, Douglas had to stop and pick every flower in sight. He peered into each blossom through a glass lens that he wore around his neck and then pulled the blossom apart. He showed me their sepals, petals, anthers, and stamens. These were all foreign words to me, and I didn't care to learn them. He talked about plants being in different families as if they were people and greeted each new one like a lost child that needed to be brought back into its circle of relatives.

"This yellow one is in the parsley family," he told me, as he placed it in the vasculum I was still carrying. "See how the flowers form an umbrella? And this one is a lily—the parts are in threes."

Meantime, Doctor Scouler was waving his net at every passing insect. Poor William Clark was torn between wanting to hurry his guests along and being pleased that they were so interested in his island, whereas I was impatient because I had a thousand questions that I couldn't ask William Clark.

When we reached the grove of gnarled old fruit trees, Douglas finally raised his eyes from the ground.

"Pears . . . peaches . . . and surely this is a quince! These vines that are crawling over everything are figs. And this pink fruit looks like some new kind of strawberry. "

"How do you know all these fruit trees?" Clark asked.

"I learned about them from William Beattie when I was a young boy. He was the gardener at Scone Palace, which had the best orchard in all of Scotland. And the best vegetable and flower gardens, too. People came from miles away just to see them."

"You lived in a palace?" Clark stared at Douglas, wide-eyed.

"No! No!" he answered, shaking his head. "I grew up in a stonemason's cottage not much bigger than your hut! When I was eleven I was apprenticed to Beattie. I learned more from him than I ever did at school. But maybe I was more willing to learn. I never gave school much of a chance."

And school never gave *me* a chance, I was thinking.

Clark then took us farther up the hillside to an old fort that had been built by the Spaniards years ago. I thought he was going to show us sturdy buildings, where I could find shelter, but either time or vandals had reduced the fort to a few broken-down walls and piles of stone. The only thing that had been spared was an old round oven. It measured about seven feet across, and some small, blue pigeons were using it as a nesting place. Douglas said that the eggs would make good eating. That might be worth knowing.

And so the day passed. A mostly wasted day, as far as *my* plans went.

The following day was worse. I had to stay on board to help Charlie clean and salt down a mess of rock codfish that Larry had caught. Charlie promised I'd get to go ashore again the next morning. He assured me there'd be plenty of time to visit the island. Captain Hanwell wanted to make some repairs to the ship, and we still needed more fresh food. We'd be riding anchor for at least three more days.

So that day I contented myself with smuggling a supply of ship's biscuits and some dried fruit back to my hammock. I tied my loot in a square of canvas, ready to take it ashore in the basket that Charlie and I were hoping to fill with the pink strawberries Douglas had told him about. And we were to look for figs as well.

My present plan—for what it was worth—was to head for the abandoned orchard with my basket of supplies. Then I'd wait for the chance to slip unnoticed into the woods above the clearing, where I'd hide among the trees until the ship sailed. The forest looked dense there. But I still didn't know how long William Clark and the Spaniards were going to be around. And would they be friends or foes?

That evening, David Douglas burst into the galley, dragging a live female goat. He'd taken Clark some vegetable seeds so he could plant them and have fresh vegetables the next time he came to the island. (Unless I've eaten them all, I thought!) Douglas had also given Clark one of his coats. The goat was in payment for Douglas' generosity, but Doctor Scouler said he'd regret it when he was shivering through next winter in the Columbia country.

"Is it one of Robinson Crusoe's goats?" Charlie asked with a chuckle.

"I hope she's younger than that!" Douglas laughed. "Can we have her for dinner on Christmas Day?"

"We will indeed!" Charlie answered. "She'll make a welcome change from lobscouse."

Poor goat! Christmas was just a week away.

That night, sleep wouldn't come. I had too much on my mind. The poor doomed goat. And what would *I* be eating on Christmas Day? Would I be eating alone? Or would I be eating roast beef with Clark and the Spaniards?

I finally drifted off to sleep only to be wakened by the familiar sounds of the ship—the snap of the sails and the shouts of the crew. It took me a few moments to figure out what was out of place. We shouldn't be moving!

I tumbled out of my hammock and scrambled up to the deck. The wind was blowing hard, and it was not yet light. The deck was swarming with sailors. Bo'sun Black was barking orders. The *William and Ann* was no longer riding anchor. She was racing northward, a strong southeasterly filling her sails.

"Here, grab this rope," Alisdair yelled, seeing me standing around doing nothing.

"What's going on?" I asked. "Charlie said we'd be at anchor for three more days."

"With the wind coming up, the Captain gave orders to head for deep water."

"Will we be going back to Juan Fernandez?"

"By the time this blows itself out, we'll be too far north."

"What about the food we were going to take on? What about the repairs to the ship?"

My insides were in a turmoil, and not because of the pitching deck. I was so filled with black despair that I actually hoped that the soul of the dead albatross was riding the wind, trying to claim the *William and Ann*.

# CHAPTER 6

*Latitude 27 degrees, south*
*December 25, 1824*

As Christmas Day drew to a close, the crew was in a rowdy mood. We had dined well on Douglas' goat, and the Captain had ordered a double ration of grog. Some of the sailors were harking back to Christmases past, while others were singing and stamping their feet to the rhythm of Larry Flett's fiddle. I was standing off by myself, my back against the port rail.

The only other person nearby was David Douglas. As usual, his nose was in a book. Every now and then, he picked up his quill pen and made a few notes on the page, but I was hardly aware of him, lost as I was in the music of Larry's fiddle. It took me back to the Orkney Islands. They didn't mark Christmas there, but New Year's more than made up for it. The *ceilidhs*, the storytelling, the singing, and the cozy warmth of the peat fire.

The music changed tempo, as Larry moved into an Orkney lament.

Suddenly, Douglas called out to me. "Sandy, you should read this!" he said. I blinked at the book he was holding in his outstretched hand. "It tells about your lark — how it draws people away from its nest by pretending to have a broken wing."

"I can't read it," I said, brushing the book aside. "I never learned how!"

The words had tumbled out of my mouth, and now there was no calling them back.

"You don't know how to read?" Douglas asked. He sounded more puzzled than surprised.

"No, I don't! I never had the chance to learn. I never went to school!"

I shouted out the words as if it were somehow Douglas' fault. Why couldn't he just leave me alone?

"Why did they sign you on to help in the store then?" he asked, still sounding puzzled. "Won't you have to be able to read and write to help with the records?"

"I can write my name," I said. "I'm not stupid!"

"Let's see you do it!" He handed me his quill, as if he didn't believe me.

I snatched it and wrote *Alexander Ross* in the margin of the last page of his book.

Taking the book back, he merely glanced at my name and then said, "Nine different letters—and there are twenty-six in the alphabet. That means you already know more than a third of the letters, Sandy. I could teach you to read and write in no time."

My anger leaked away.

"Could you really do that?" I whispered. At that moment, I swear I wasn't thinking of how this would solve my problem when I reached the Hudson Bay's post. It was more that it was something I had always hungered to do.

"I don't see why not!"

"Now?" I asked.

"Let's go down to the cabin," Douglas said. "It's quieter there! And we'll have the lantern light."

He acted as if inviting me down to his cabin was just a small thing. I followed him, fleetingly hoping that the dead albatross wouldn't be lying on his bunk. It wasn't, but the cabin did smell a bit rank. Piles of paper, weighted down with books, lay all over the floor.

Douglas cleared off a section of his small table and told me to sit down. It didn't take me long to master the twenty-six letters, but then I found where the difficulty in reading lies. There is no end of ways to combine those letters so that each time they form a different word. I soon felt discouraged. And then angry. It would take me forever to sort them all out. But Douglas was patient.

"How do you know a fulmar from a seagull?" he asked.

"I just know," I answered, shrugging.

"But tell me how," he persisted. "They look alike—mostly white and about the same size—yet you say you can tell them apart."

"I know them from their shape and from the way they fly."

"And so it is with words. You don't need to look at each letter to know a word any more than you need to look at each feather to know a bird. You learn to see the pattern like a pattern of feathers. And then you see the shape of the word, and you know it from the way the sense of it carries you across the page."

He opened the bird book again and pointed to a word. Then he asked me what I could see in it. I sat there feeling stupid, but when he covered the first five letters, the last part of the word jumped out at me—*ross*. My last name! Then Douglas showed me the first two letters and I saw that the word started out with the same letters as Alexander.

"So what does it say?" Douglas asked.

I glanced at the picture and then turned to Douglas with a wide grin.

"It says *albatross!*"

I had read my first word!

"It's a sign of good luck to share so much of your name with a bird!" Douglas said, laughing. I believed him. Especially when he showed me a sandpiper and how its name contained most of the letters in *Sandy*.

Then Douglas reached for one of his botany books, and I picked out the names of the flowers I knew on Orkney—buttercup and sea thrift. Other words hid within the names—like *butter* and *cup* and *sea* and *thrift*. It was like uncovering treasure. And even within these names were other words that no one gave much thought to—*but* and *if* and *up*.

Learning to read was not as hard as finding the time to do it. With Christmas over, it was back to helping in the galley or wherever someone needed me, but I soon began to discover words everywhere—on the cargo in the hold and on the storage vats in the ship's larder. I could practice my reading while I was working.

In spite of what Douglas had said about not looking at each feather, I found that sometimes the best way to get at a word was from sounding out each letter, though it was confusing how letters changed their sound depending on what they stood next to. People were like that, too, I'd noticed. Charlie Crabtree was a far different sounding man standing next to Captain Hanwell than when he was Old Crab, who swore at me when I was slow in doing his bidding. Now that I had found some words to read in the galley, I minded his swearing less!

And now that I was learning to read, the letter that I was to give to the Chief Factor was no longer like a lead weight around my neck. For the first time since we left Gravesend, the New World beckoned.

*Delphinium menziesii* (Menzies' larkspur)

# *Traveling Companions*

## by John Scouler
### Ship's Doctor

*In the afternoon in company with Mr. Douglass
I made a short visit to the shore. The first [plant]
we collected on North American continent was
the charming* Gaultheria Shallon, *in an excellent
condition.*

Dr. John Scouler's Journal
April 9, 1825

*Saturday the 9th in company with Mr Scouler I
went on shore on Cape Disappointment as the ship
could not proceed up the river on consequence of
heavy rains and thick fogs. On stepping on the shore*
Gaultheria Shallon *was the first plant I took in my
hands. . . . It grows most luxuriantly on the margins
of woods, particularly near the ocean.*

David Douglas' Journal
April 1825

# CHAPTER 7

*The Galapagos Islands and north*
*January to February 1825*

When the New Year dawned in 1825, I had been the ship's
doctor on the *William and Ann* for more than five months, and
everyone was still hale and hearty. One of the big surprises
of the previous year—besides finding myself in charge of the
health of a shipload of sailors—was the discovery that the
famous botanist, David Douglas, would be my cabin mate.

Douglas and I had first met four years earlier while attending
Professor Hooker's botany lectures in Glasgow. I was sixteen at
the time and was just starting my medical studies. I don't think
Douglas even saw me at those early lectures, but I noticed him
right away. He was so old—all of twenty-one years! (At sixteen,
five years is a bigger gap than it is at twenty.) I am ashamed
to admit that it was Douglas' clothes that really set him apart
in my mind. He always wore the same threadbare jacket and
shabby boots. As an undergardener at the Botanic Gardens, I
suppose he couldn't afford to dress any better.

Apparently, Professor Hooker looked past Douglas' clothes
and his lowly occupation. He invited him to his house for dinner
and took him on several botanical expeditions to the Highlands.
He admired the gardener's zeal for collecting—and his single-
mindedness. Hooker was actually responsible for Douglas being
on the *William and Ann*. After one of their collecting trips, he
wrote to Joseph Sabine, the Secretary of the Royal Horticultural
Society, telling him that Douglas had all the qualities needed
to be a successful plant collector in far-off lands. He stopped
at nothing when it came to obtaining a new plant for science—

a quality that was borne out many times in our adventures together!

Luckily, I had put all my prejudices behind me long before we became cabin mates. By then I knew that Douglas would be an ideal companion. We both loved natural history, and he was generous about sharing everything he knew. But by January, the novelty of the journey was wearing off. The cabin, which had seemed quite roomy at first, felt crowded and dirty. Every square inch of space was taken up with specimens we had collected along the way—birds, shells, rocks, seaweed, and flowers. Papers and plant presses were piled on every flat surface.

And now, Sandy Ross, the cabin boy, had added himself to the clutter! The boy was always underfoot. Whenever I returned to our quarters, I would find him crouched in a corner, laboring to write a few words on a scrap of paper or frowning over the pages of an open book. Somehow, he had signed on to keep records in the Company store even though all he could write was his own name!

When Douglas found this out, he decided to take a hand in the lad's education. I could not see why he did not let Sandy face the consequences of his actions, but I have to admit I was impressed by the lad's tenacity. Every minute he could scrape from his duties in the galley was spent trying to read the names in Douglas' botany books. His face positively glowed when he came across a flower that grew on the Orkney Islands.

I suppose I should not have been so hard on Sandy. In a way, I had signed on under false pretenses, too. I had always wanted to travel to faraway places to collect natural history specimens, so when I was offered the post of ship's doctor on the *William and Ann,* I jumped at the chance. I would have all the time in the world for collecting.

I never gave a thought to what my obligations might be as a doctor. I had just finished my medical training and had never actually treated a patient, but it was only after we were out at sea that I began to worry about what I would do if there were a serious accident on board or an outbreak of ship's fever. So far, my luck had held. All I had been called to do was lance a few boils and administer eucalyptus oil for coughs. The worst thing

I had had to deal with was when the albatross took a slice out of Bo'sun Black's leg. Luckily, it didn't go septic.

All my worries and irritations fell away a week later when we approached the Galapagos Islands. Douglas and I had heard that the place was a naturalist's paradise. Though on first sight, James Island fell a bit short of our expectations.

The dark volcanic rock supported none of the lush vegetation we had pictured on a tropical island. But we soon discovered that the animals made up for the lack of bright flowers. Lizards the color of fire basked on black rocks, and the birds were so unused to people that they landed on our shoulders. We could take any specimens we needed with a blow from a stick. When Douglas let Sandy try out his gun, the pigeon the boy wanted to bring down took refuge by perching on the muzzle. It is impossible to shoot a bird while it is sitting on your gun!

As far as we knew, the island was uninhabited, but the land, which rose steeply from the shore, was marked by a network of narrow roads. They seemed to have been made with a purpose. When I set off to explore one of them, Sandy came along, too. We had not gone more than a hundred yards when we caught up with Larry Flett and a grizzled old sailor named Jim, staring down at a big, round rock.

On seeing Sandy, Flett challenged him with a mischievous grin. "Let's see you climb onto this stone!"

The stone was smooth and low enough that all Sandy had to do was step up onto it. But when he did—to his surprise—the rock grew legs and walked out from under him. The lad slipped off, and the two men roared with laughter at the expression of surprise on his face.

"It's alive! What on earth is it?" Sandy gasped.

"A tortoise!" Jim answered.

"That's no tortoise! Charlie Crabtree says we'll be eating tortoise meat for the rest of the voyage, but no one's going to eat an animal that looks like a rock!"

"It's a tortoise, right enough!" Jim insisted. "You're not a true sailor till you've feasted on a chunk of tortoise flesh on roasted breastplate—a real mouth-watering treat! Tender as a plump chicken!"

"We'd never eat a beast like this where I come from!" Sandy answered.

In his eyes, that settled the matter. The Orkney Islands were his standard for how things should be the world over.

The tortoise was on its way to a waterhole. I learned later that the paths that criss-crossed the island had been worn into the rock by generations of these animals looking for water. They live down by the shore eating grass and cactus plants, but every now and then they plod up to the springs in the uplands to drink their fill.

The waterhole was a wonderful sight. Around a dozen tortoises were drinking greedily. Others were wallowing in the mud on the far side of the pond. One — he looked like the grandfather of them all — had his head under the water and was swallowing in great gulps. When his thirst was finally quenched, he raised his head and stared at us for several minutes with unblinking eyes. Then he lumbered off back down the path.

"I wager that big fellow weighs four hundred pounds," old Jim said. "Not that anyone reckons their weight in pounds. We judge 'em by how many sailors it takes to heave 'em on board. We stack 'em upside down on the deck, so they can't walk away. We'll need enough meat to keep us going for the rest of the voyage."

Douglas and I were too busy collecting plants and snaring birds to take part in the tortoise roundup. Besides, it didn't look like it was much sport. When anyone came near, they did not run but simply sank to the ground, pulling in their legs. The hard part was taking them down to the shore, carrying the huge creatures over loose lava under the broiling sun.

Once we were out at sea again, torrential tropical rains set in and did not let up for twelve days. We soon collected enough water in a sheet of sailcloth to more than satisfy our needs. The sailors grumbled about all the wasted effort of carrying the heavy casks down from the springs on the Galapagos. But the overabundance of water gave the men the chance to wash themselves and their clothes, and they were all in a lively mood.

Douglas and I took no part in the fun. We were too worried about the fate of our collections to enjoy the warm downpour. Especially Douglas. He had forty different kinds of birds that needed to be skinned and preserved. There was no way to dry the skins on the deck, and we had no room to spread them out in the cabin. And Sandy Ross still sat scrunched in a corner. Douglas had given him the task of writing labels so he could practice his handwriting. And that's all it was—practice. The labels were not needed.

Most of the skins mildewed or rotted. Out of the forty bird specimens, only one booby was worth keeping. It was a large seabird with blue webbed feet. I remember Sandy laughing at that word as he wrote the label. *Booby.*

Douglas' plant collection fared no better. The papers he used to press the plants sucked up moisture from the humid air. One hundred and thirty-five out of one hundred and seventy-five specimens went moldy. The poor man hunched over his journal, recording how terrible it was to have such a miserable collection from a place where everything, even the most trifling particle, would have been of interest back in England.

I didn't say much. I would be homeward-bound later in the year and would have another chance to collect on these strange islands, but Sandy tried to console Douglas by pointing out that the people in England could see finer blossoms among the weeds along the roadsides than all those dry prickly shrubs that grew on the Galapagos. It did not help. Douglas just kept up a dreary lament that he might never have the chance to see those plants again.

The next leg of the journey was uneventful. We reached the latitude of the mighty Columbia River in mid-February, but then a wild storm kept us from putting in to shore. The Captain said it would be asking for disaster to cross the sandbar at the river's mouth with the wind blowing so hard. The only course open to us was to head out to sea.

Day after day, week after week, we waited for the wind to drop. The cold, lashing rain and pounding waves were a thousand times worse than anything we had seen earlier, even on our way around the Cape. It gnawed at our souls to know that the Great River of the West was so close, yet out of reach. We had eaten the last of the tortoise meat, and Crabtree was worried that we were going to run out of food. Fresh water was not a problem, except that most of the time the wind was so strong that the rain fell sideways as the buckets rattled across the slippery deck.

Sandy still came to our cabin under the pretext of wanting to continue his lessons, even though the rolling and pitching of the ship made reading and writing impossible. I think he wanted to get away from Charlie Crabtree's outbursts. We tried to divert ourselves by talking about the adventures that lay ahead, but mostly we found ourselves thinking back to the people we had left behind. How different my upbringing was from Douglas'! Father had mapped out my life from the time I learned to walk, always pointing me toward a career in medicine. I was expected to join the family practice. Accepting the post as surgeon and naturalist on the *William and Ann* was the most defiant thing I had ever done.

After hearing Douglas and Sandy talk about their early years, I could see what had prompted Douglas to take the lad under his wing. Sandy had lost his right to a share in the kelp harvest when his father died, forcing him to move in with his Aunt Agnes and a houseful of young cousins.

Douglas had his own story about being at the mercy of a landowner.

"I was born in Perthshire in the old village of Scone next to Scone Palace," he said, raising his voice to be heard over the din of the storm. "When I was two years old, the Earl of Mansfield added a new wing to the Palace. The windows looked out toward our village, and that spoiled the view from the Earl's sitting-room window, so he ordered the whole village to be relocated a few miles away! The parish church was moved stone by stone and then rebuilt.

"It was a sad thing for my mother to be uprooted like that. But in the end, it turned out to be good for our family. My father's a stonemason. Building new houses for everyone in the village and moving the church provided him with steady work for years. We were soon well enough off that my brothers and I could go to the parish school at Kinnoull. John and Robert were good students, though I never really took to being shut up in a classroom."

Douglas paused as the ship listed to an impossible angle. By now, everything that could move had been bolted down.

"I swear I learned more on the six-mile walk back and forth to school than I ever did in class," Douglas continued, when the brig righted herself. "I knew every flower along the way. Some days I'd be so intent on looking for birds' nests that I'd forget to go altogether! Or I'd get there late and be caned for it. Later on, when I could see a use for some of my lessons, I was a better student. I took to Latin quite easily."

"You know your Latin well," I agreed. "And it has stood you in good stead. Doctor Hooker liked the way you could toss out those plant names."

"I wouldn't be here if it wasn't for Doctor Hooker," Douglas answered.

"He set all our souls on fire with his love for the wildflowers on the moors and along the hedgerows," I said. "Remember how it was standing room only in that dingy little lecture hall. It was hardly bigger than a dog kennel!"

"And those trips he led to the Highlands! Walking thirty miles a day sharpened our appetites for the evening meals of bread and cheese and a pint of ale! Then we would press our flowers and label them. After a few hours sleep in a hay loft, we would be on our way again at daybreak."

At that moment, our happy recollections were interrupted by an urgent knock on the cabin door, followed by a chorus of loud voices.

"Doctor! Doctor Scouler! There's been an accident! You're needed on the deck."

Those were the words I had been dreading ever since we left England!

My mouth went dry as I picked up my black bag and followed the excited men to the upper deck. It was slick with rain. Near the mast, Bo'sun Black lay sprawled on his side, with his left leg at an awkward angle. I could not tell if he had fallen from the rigging or had just slipped on the deck, but it did not take medical training to see that the leg was badly broken.

Kneeling down, I gently probed the leg with my fingers. Black screamed and tried to pull away. The break was in the middle third of the femur, and the upper part of the bone was nearly poking through the skin. With help, I moved the poor man to a cot, and there I managed — in spite of the tossing and pitching of the ship and Black's piercing cries — to bring the pieces of bone together, just as I had seen it done in the surgery in Glasgow. After I splinted and bandaged his leg, I gave Black opium to calm him.

I was pleased with how the operation had gone, but the raging storm undid my good work. Four weeks after the accident, on March 25, I wrote in my journal:

*The effect of this weather on the boatswain has been such as to spoil the sanguine hopes I had entertained of a perfect cure. The pain has been so great at times to oblige me to get up during the night to relax the dressings for some time & to give opium.*

The weather improved, and on the night of the twenty-eighth, I was able to write:

*For the last three days the weather has been more moderate & has produced a beneficial effect on my patient's comfort & spirits.*

Five days later, we were close enough to land to make out the dim outline of Cape Disappointment. Captain Hanwell ordered the crew to shorten the sail. Tomorrow we would cross the bar.

The next day, a steady breeze carried us within four miles of the river. Then Cape Disappointment lived up to its name, as a violent storm from the west forced us out to sea again.

Two days later, the wind dropped and the clouds thinned. When the sun rose, the *William and Ann* was forty miles out, and everyone on board was hoping that this time luck would be with us. Douglas and I took the soundings as the ship inched slowly forward. Three hours later, we lay at anchor in Baker Bay on the north bank of the great Columbia River. A new chapter of our adventures was about to begin.

Captain Hanwell fired the cannon to announce our safe arrival to the factor at Fort George seven miles upriver. He waited for an answering shot.

None came.

Several more shots were fired.

Still no answer.

That night, Douglas and I whispered to one another in the quiet stillness of the cabin. We had grown so used to the constant tossing of the ship that it was hard to sleep. We wondered why no one at Fort George had answered the gun salute. We had heard enough tales during the last nine months to set our imaginations on fire. There could be many reasons for the silence.

Plagues . . . massacres . . . grizzly bears . . .

# CHAPTER 8

*The Columbia River*
*April 1825*

Fog and rain held us captive in Baker's Bay for several days. Then, on the ninth day of April, our first meeting with the inhabitants of this mysterious new land broke the boredom. Around mid-morning, while I was pacing the deck, I saw several big canoes looming up out of the mist. When three of them drew alongside the ship, I could see that the men were armed with bows and arrows, a good supply of daggers, and even one or two long-stemmed rifles. So I was surprised when Captain Hanwell ordered the crew to lower a rope ladder.

I edged back behind the mast when around twenty men and women scrambled up the ladder. But it turned out they were mostly interested in trading. They offered us an assortment of woven hats, dried fish, and wrinkled berries, all talking in their own language, with a few English and French words thrown in. And plenty of gestures. When they produced a basket of potatoes, they really caught our interest. Food from home! We had not seen a potato in months.

They were not big people. The tallest was no more than five and a half feet. Their hair was long, straight, and black, and none of the men had beards. Some had flat, sloping foreheads. They wore conical hats made of something that looked like straw, and the men had skin robes thrown loosely over their shoulders. The women also wore skin robes, and petticoats made from lengths of some sort of cord woven closely together. But their most notable feature was the shells and beads that dangled from their pierced ears and noses. One couple stood out from the rest because of their European-type clothes. The man was dressed in a scarlet coat with brass buttons, the woman in a piece of red cloth.

With help from some of the crew who had been here before, we gradually understood that all of the white men—the natives called them King George men—had recently left the fort and gone upriver. That was why nobody had answered the ship's cannon fire two days earlier. We also gathered that someone from their village had been murdered by an Indian from a nearby tribe and that they were preparing for battle.

The morning ended on a convivial note when Charlie Crabtree served up a feast of bread and molasses. Our visitors gobbled up everything in sight and then asked for more. They enjoyed Charlie's bread as much as we enjoyed their potatoes when we had them later that afternoon with a cup of tea.

That same day, Captain Hanwell gave Douglas and me permission to go ashore. Words cannot begin to describe how we felt when we finally set foot in the New World! The first plant that welcomed us was *Gaultheria shallon*, commonly called salal—a shrub with beautiful dark, shiny leaves. Even in the wild, it grows so uniformly that it looks as if it has been planted by a careful gardener. Douglas reached out and touched the clusters of pink-tinged, bell-shaped flowers. I could tell that he was picturing salal bordering the paths of an English garden.

We fought our way through the brush into the forest. Looking upward, our faces sallow in the filtered light, we were overwhelmed by the size of the trees. Massive trunks of hemlock, spruce, pine, and cedar supported a green roof over our heads. Some of the trunks must have measured fifty feet around. Mosses and lichens hung from the branches like tapestries, and the ferns grew shoulder high. The ground was carpeted with a deep, soft layer of spongy needles.

The trees seemed to have been growing there forever, but there was no way of knowing their age. You could not fell a tree that size to count its rings! They were surely safe from man's destruction, but here and there we saw evidence of nature's violence—a huge trunk melting into the forest floor with young saplings sprouting up along its length.

For a long time, we did nothing but stand and stare, worshipping in nature's cathedral.

Three days later, the *William and Ann* made her way up the Columbia River to Fort George with a lively escort of Indian canoes. I was surprised to find that the fort was built entirely of wood—both the buildings and the palisade around them. I could not help thinking stone would have been a better choice, even though wood was plentiful. The inside of the building was more like a trading post than my idea of a fort. Stores and warehouses occupied the west side of the enclosure, and small huts had been built against the palisade. To the south was a large building where the Hudson's Bay men had lived before they moved upriver.

Doctor John McLoughlin, the Chief Factor, had taken everyone with him to the new fort, leaving Alexander McKenzie to welcome us. He told us he had already sent a messenger to let Doctor McLoughlin know that the supply ship had arrived safely, and he assured us that the factor would come down as soon as he heard the news.

The new fort, which was eighty miles upriver, was called Fort Vancouver. It was named in honor of George Vancouver, the British captain who had sailed his ship, the *Discovery,* into the Great River of the West back in 1792. It was just bad luck that stormy weather had kept the *Discovery* from going farther upriver. That autumn, an American sea captain, Robert Gray, crossed the bar and named the river the Columbia after *his* ship.

But nobody wanted a history lesson. All we were interested in was what was happening now. Especially among the Indians. It was clear that the murder we had heard about was big news. When we asked Mister McKenzie about it, he explained in a resigned voice that fights often broke out among the tribes. "Though this time it involves Concomly," he told us. "He's one of the big chiefs along the river, so it could turn nasty. A while ago, two of Concomly's sons fell sick, and a neighboring chief offered to cure them by singing over them. Unfortunately, both the young men died. Concomly blamed their deaths on the chief's bad magic and ordered his remaining son to kill the chief—which he did. Now the chief's tribe wants revenge.

Concomly's going to visit his sons' graves tomorrow. They happen to be right next to the murdered chief's village, so there's sure to be trouble."

Instead of returning to the *William and Ann* with the others, Douglas and I set off on a plant-hunting expedition, following a stream that took us up into the forest on a hill behind the fort. We had not gone far when we came upon a lodge, solidly built of split cedar logs. It looked big enough to be a meeting hall — or maybe it belonged to more than one family. Curious as to what it was like inside, we walked right in without a thought.

We did not get far.

We were met by two men with drawn daggers. This clearly was not the time to test our ability to communicate. We turned and ran, retracing our way as best we could. Although no one followed us, we agreed that we had done enough collecting that day and made straight for the fort. The encounter made me nervous, but Douglas shrugged it off. He said that we had been impolite. After all, we would never walk into a house in Scotland without an invitation.

The next day, from the safety of the ship, I watched a group of warriors clad in elk-skin cloaks march down from the direction of the fort to the beach. Their feet were locked in an identical rhythm, and they yelled as they fired shots into the air. Their faces were streaked with black and red and yellow paint. Once they reached the beach, they formed a circle and danced to the music of rattling shells. Their war cries filled the air. I was glad for the stretch of water between the ship and the shore, but I could tell from Sandy Ross' face that he would not have minded being out there dancing with them!

Doctor McLoughlin arrived at Fort George a few days later. McKenzie had spoken of him in such glowing terms that I did not see how he could live up to all that praise. I was ready to feel let down. But when the Chief Factor stepped out from his dugout canoe — all six-foot-four of him — his shoulder-length white hair blowing in the wind, I fell under his spell.

He greeted us in a strong, melodious voice. Almost the first thing he did was to single out David Douglas.

"Ah, our honored scientific guest!" he said, shaking Douglas' outstretched hand vigorously. "You can count on us to help you in every way we can."

Douglas stood there, flushed and wordless, as happy as if he had just discovered a new species of fir tree!

The new recruits were introduced in turn. Then Sandy approached the Chief Factor and handed over a sealed letter. He stood there, first on one foot and then on the other, fidgeting nervously, while he watched Doctor McLoughlin read the document.

"So you're trapper Ross' young brother?" the factor said, looking at Sandy with considerable interest. "You've missed finding him here at Fort George by a year or two! There's a fair stretch of miles between you now. He spent last winter over at the Flathead Post, but I doubt he'll still be there now that spring is here."

"Would that be John or Angus?" Sandy asked.

"John or Angus?" McLoughlin repeated. "I'm talking about *Alexander* Ross."

"You *must* mean John or Angus," Sandy broke in. "*I'm* Alexander Ross! Though people mostly call me Sandy."

McLoughlin looked puzzled for a moment and then said kindly. "I'm sorry, lad! I was confused. Our Alexander Ross couldn't be your brother! Besides having the same name, he's too old. He came over from Scotland twenty years ago — before you were even born. Ah, well, if you're half the man your namesake is, you'll do well here. I think I'll put you in charge of the pigs. They've been giving us a lot of trouble!"

Sandy stared at the ground, biting his lip and fighting back tears. His hopes had been raised for a moment, only to be dashed. And after putting all that effort into learning to read, he was to tend the pigs! But he was young, I told myself. He still had lots of time to make his way.

When Doctor McLoughlin returned to Fort Vancouver, he took David Douglas along with him. I knew I would be going upriver in a week or two with the crew from the *William and Ann*, but I could not help being a bit jealous of Douglas. He would be out there exploring this great new country while the rest of us unloaded and organized the mountain of cargo that was to keep the fort going for the next year. We also had to ready the ship for a trading trip up the coast.

By April 29, our tasks were complete. That night, I wrote in my journal:

> *This morning I set out on a visit to Ft. Vancouver. . . . Our party consisted of 5 canoes, superintended by Mr. McKay. As the wind was favourable we made rapid progress & in the evening we slept at Oak Point, 30 miles from Ft. George.*

The dugouts were impressive boats. From my seat in the stern, our canoe looked nearly as long as the *William and Ann*. The backs of the six Indian oarsmen glistened with sweat as the swift, quiet strokes of their paddles sent ripples across the surface of the water. The ash trees and willows that edged the riverbank glittered fresh green against a backdrop of dark pines. A great blue heron, standing motionless in the shallows, waited patiently for its next meal.

We traveled all day without stopping.

At dusk, the oarsmen beached the canoes, dragged them onto the bank, and unloaded the cargo. They would serve as shelter for the night. I wandered off to explore the marshy ground near the river, while the Indians built a fire and set about roasting an enormous sturgeon. Long after all the King George men had their fill, the Indians were still eating. Even taking into account that they had been rowing against the current all day, I was impressed by their appetites. They ate their way through the entire night. Meanwhile, I tried to make myself comfortable under an upturned canoe. It kept off the rain, which was now falling steadily, but I spent a long, uneasy night listening to unexplained noises that came from the forest.

The next day was taken up with sealing two canoes that had sprung leaks. This was done with pine resin. The process, called gumming, was a requirement on every long trip. The delay gave me a chance to add more plants to my collection. I pounced on each new find, hoping it was something Douglas had not already discovered.

We reached Fort Vancouver on the fifth day. When we pulled in on the north bank of the river, I stood there wide-eyed, taking in the huge stretch of grassland with magnificent snowcapped peaks in the distance. Doctor McLoughlin could not have chosen a better place to build. The site was worthy of a manor house.

A noisy group of men, mostly dressed in skin jerkins and leather leggings, was waiting for us. Orders came from all directions.

"Unload the cargo!'

"Move everything up to the fort!"

"*Vite! Vite!*"

Balancing a box of my belongings on my shoulder, I strode up the gently sloping ground, knee-deep in grass and flowers. The palisade around the fort — nearly three times my height — was already complete. Inside the enclosure, chaos reigned. Cattle, pigs, and chickens wandered among a scattering of huts and tents. A horse-drawn plough was turning over the soil in the far corner. Several bigger buildings stood half finished. The blow of hammers and the rasping sound of a saw were almost drowned out by the wail of bagpipes. A Scottish piper was giving us our official welcome!

When the men had finished unloading the canoes and stacking all the crates, Doctor McLoughlin emerged from his half-completed house and started giving more orders. Most of the new recruits would be working on the land. He warned us that missing the growing season would mean no food next winter, so planting crops and caring for the cattle were even more important than putting up more buildings.

While I was looking around for Douglas, I had an interesting conversation with Edward Ermatinger, one of the Company clerks. He told me about Doctor McLoughlin's ambitions for the fort along with a few facts that I was able to combine with my own observations when I wrote my journal entry that evening:

*Ft. Vancouver is built on the same plan as the other fort, but is not so large. Its situation is far more pleasant than that of Ft. George. It is situated in the middle of a beautiful prairie, containing about 300 acres of excellent land, on which potatoes & other vegetables are cultivated; while a large plain between the fort and river affords abundance of pasture to 120 horses, besides other cattle.*

When I finally found Douglas, he was inside his own tent changing the papers in his flower press. He had been too busy to come looking for me, but when he saw me he greeted me with great affection. It turned out, however, that he was mostly excited to see me because my arrival meant that the supplies from the ship were here.

Once I assured him that we had indeed brought papers for his plant press, he showed me his recent finds and then began to tell me about his trip to Menzies Island out in the Columbia River. A botanist's paradise, he called it. The island was named after Archibald Menzies, the doctor on George Vancouver's ship, the *Discovery*.

"You won't believe the profusion of flowers!" he said. "I can't wait to show you!"

Less than an hour later, with our collecting gear on our backs, we headed down to the riverbank, where Douglas had cached a small canoe that Doctor McLoughlin had lent him.

The island was just as Douglas had described it—an untamed garden, sparkling with summer blossoms. Surrounded by all those flowers, I could not help thinking that God had been lavish, creating so many different kinds of plants in a place with so few people to enjoy them.

As we peered through our magnifying lenses at arrangements of petals and sepals and anthers, I soon began to appreciate the depth of Douglas' botanical knowledge. On an earlier trip to New York, he had collected a large number of plant specimens from this continent, but it was the months he had spent in London studying Menzies' collection and his description of plants that helped him the most. I do not think there was a botanical book he had not read. And he had visited gardens all around London, viewing plants from earlier expeditions.

So it was no surprise that he could look at a small blue flower and announce that it was a new kind of forget-me-not. We decided to name it *Myosotis Hookeri* as a tribute to our old professor. Douglas honored Joseph Sabine, the secretary of the Horticultural Society, by naming a pretty pink flower *Phlox Sabina*. He suggested *Mimulus Scouleri* for a small monkey flower. We both knew only too well that some botanist in a dusty office in London would change the names, but for now we could call them whatever pleased us!

On our way back from the river, we stopped to admire the pig enclosure that Sandy Ross was building with the help of Na-Wam, an Indian from the fort. They had started by laying a branch flat on the ground and placing the end of the next branch over it at a wide angle. A third branch matched the direction of the first one. When they had laid a zigzag line of branches all around the enclosure, they were ready to start on the next layer.

A few days later, Sandy proudly invited us to see the completed enclosure and the pigpen. It was finished just in time. One of the pigs had already produced eight little piglets.

"Raising pigs is going to be easy!" Sandy bragged.

The following day, there were only three piglets.

"*Chakchak*," Na-wam said, pointing to the sky.

"An eagle," Sandy explained.

The pen would need a roof and a door.


All too soon, it was time to return to the *William and Ann* for the coastal trading trip with the Nootka Indians. In the few short weeks I had spent at the fort, the Columbia had become a different river. Settlements had sprung up along the banks, and hundreds of Indians — men, women, and children — were catching and drying salmon and sturgeon. I traded two inches of tobacco for a couple of salmon weighing about thirty-five pounds each. Two fish for a penny each! In England, they would have cost me three or four pounds.

The rest of the summer passed uneventfully. I was lucky in that none of the crew suffered injuries or sickness. The scenery along the coast was majestic, but Captain Hanwell never let us leave the ship. He worried about trouble with Indians. Of course, trading suffered. And so did collecting.

All I had to show for the journey was a few birds. I could not help thinking how Douglas' collection must be growing as he explored the Columbia country. But I still had one more visit to Fort Vancouver to look forward to. We needed to pick up a cargo of animal furs to take back to England. And I would be taking some of Douglas' botanical treasures back to the Horticultural Society in London.

# CHAPTER 9

*Fort Vancouver*
*October 1825*

As soon as we arrived at Fort Vancouver, I went in search of David Douglas. The fort had changed over the summer. Several of the buildings — the mess hall and trading post — were more or less finished. Douglas now had a comfortable hut of cedar bark.

But no one answered my knock.

I then went looking for Sandy Ross, thinking he would know of Douglas' whereabouts. I found him scraping a beaver skin — a job he didn't seem to relish. He told me that Douglas was off on a collecting trip up the Columbia, to the country beyond the Grand Rapids.

"He's due back any day," he said. "Unless he's heard of a rare plant someplace else."

"Has the collecting been good?" I asked.

"Aye, it has!" Sandy answered. "No flower is safe from Mister Douglas! He'd climb a mountain on his hands and knees if he thought there was a saxifrage or a brown peony at the top. He's been teaching me the names of the plants that grow around here — some of them in Latin. My head's fairly burstin' with all those senseless words!"

So I settled in to wait for Douglas, making myself at home among his stacks of plant papers and boxes of seeds. His time had not been wasted! When I compared his summer with my trip up the coast, I could not help feeling a twinge of jealousy.

Douglas stumbled in a few days later. After we had greeted one another, he pulled off his boots and bathed his blistered feet. His face was scarlet and his nose was peeling, but I could tell that things were going well. He had a new confidence about him. He now preferred to travel with an Indian guide, he said. When he went along with the trappers from the fort, they set the route and the pace. And they did not always go where the flowers grew the thickest.

"I've heard you shouldn't trust the Indians," I said. "Especially in the wilderness."

I was thinking about Captain Hanwell's constant warnings.

"I get along with them," Douglas answered, with a shrug. "Some better than others. They call me Olla-piska!"

"Olla-piska?"

"It means 'fire' in the Chinook jargon."

"Because of your sunburned nose?"

Douglas laughed.

"The first time my canoemen called me Olla-piska was when I was drinking a glass of Epsom salts. They saw the bubbles and thought I was drinking boiling water! When I lit my pipe by directing the sun's rays through my magnifying lens, this impressed them even more. It doesn't hurt to be good at fire magic!"

"Olla-piska!" I repeated enviously. The name had a nice sound.

"Being a good marksman gains their respect, too. While I was at Chief Cockqua's longhouse, I shot the crown out of a hat that he tossed in the air, and then I brought down an eagle on the wing."

He untied his bundle and brought out three woven hats.

"Take a look at these!" he said. "Cockqua gave them to me a few days ago. Back in July, while I was staying with him near the coast, he presented me with some baskets his daughter T'Catisa had made. When I admired his hat, he took it off his head and handed it to me, saying that I could have it. He said if I wanted more hats, T'Catisa would be happy to make them for me. When he met up with me near the Grand Rapids, he had these three hats with him. He'd come all the way from the coast to bring them to me. He also brought me huckleberry seeds I'd asked the girl to gather, because the seeds weren't ripe in July.

I rewarded him with a blanket and gave him some pins and needles and beads for his little girl."

"When you visited him, did you actually stay in his house?" I asked. I was remembering how we had been met with drawn daggers when we tried to go into the house near Fort George. And the Captain had not trusted the Nootkas enough to let us go ashore, let alone sleep in their houses.

"Cockqua did invite me to sleep in his lodge," Douglas answered. "The Clatsops were camped across the river, and he was afraid they were planning an attack. So it came down to a tough decision—a possible attack by Indians if I slept in my tent or a sure attack from fleas if I slept in Cockqua's lodge! I chose the tent! For a while, the Clatsop warriors' chanting kept me awake, but they stayed on their side of the water and I finally drifted off to sleep. That night I slept in my tent, but I mostly sleep under the stars. I just throw a blanket on the sand or under a bush when it's time for bed . . . though I don't know what my poor mother would say if she knew! Back in Scotland, she wouldn't even let us sleep with the window open because she worried about the night air! Maybe that's why in the beginning I faced the night with a sort of dread. But I'm glad to say I'm used to it by now."

That evening the entire company gathered in the almost-completed mess hall for a dinner to honor the crew of the *William and Ann*. The cooks must have worked day and night to provide us with such a feast. The polished table shone in the lamplight, and the meal was elegantly served on china plates that had come all the way from England. Doctor McLoughlin believed in keeping standards high in this distant post of the British Empire.

Once we had eaten all we could hold and knocked back a measure or two of rum, the *voyageurs* began to outdo one another with tales of their adventures. I was somewhat surprised to find that David Douglas was in big demand as a storyteller. Most of the trappers treated him with a sort of humorous respect. Even though everyone else in the room believed that risking your life for a beaver skin made more sense than risking it for a flower or a pine cone, they were still willing to listen to Douglas recite the

Latin names of the plants he had brought back from his latest excursion.

Trapper Henri Demers told about being on a trip with Douglas a few weeks earlier. He said that Douglas fell so far behind the rest of them that they had all finished their supper of dried salmon and settled down for the night before the worthy botanist crawled into the campsite on his hands and knees. He was so weary he could not stand up. He groped around fixing his supper — two partridges he had shot earlier in the day — but he fell asleep before they were cooked.

Douglas then took up the story. "I was so far gone in sleep that I didn't smell the meat burning. When I woke the next morning, there was my supper turned to ashes. Even worse, there were three holes in my kettle! I had to scour out the lid of my tinderbox to boil water for tea. There's nothing to beat a basin of tea when you're tired and discouraged. It truly is the king of all foods!"

After the tables were cleared, Edward Ermatinger brought out his flute and Larry Flett played the fiddle. In spite of all the noise and merriment, I spotted Sandy over in a corner with an open book in front of him.

"Why's the lad off by himself?" I asked Douglas.

"I think he still pines for his brothers. And he's homesick for his beloved Orkney Islands. He complains that everything is too big here — the rivers and mountains and trees and even the fish! I suppose that if you've lived all your life on an island that you can walk across in a single day, the scale of things here must seem wrong."

A few mornings later, Sandy burst into Douglas' hut. To my surprise, he was looking for me. An old Indian chief was very sick and needed a doctor! Sandy thought his name was Futillifum.

"*I* can't do anything for him," I said. I had not forgotten what had happened to the medicine man who treated Concomly's sons.

Sandy tugged at my sleeve, impatient for me to come.

"You don't know you cannot help him till you've seen what ails him," Douglas said quietly.

"But he's an Indian . . ." I trailed off.

Olla-piska, the man of fire, could see that I was afraid.

I got to my feet, saying that I supposed I could at least take a look.

As I followed Sandy through the fort, I tried to bolster myself with the thought that if the chief got better, the Indians might give me a new name. Futillifum's great white healer!

The sick chief was lying on a blanket in the shadow of the palisade surrounded by a crowd of curious onlookers. They parted to make room for us.

One glance told me that the poor man was beyond my help. There was not anything I could do. Futillifum's body was painfully thin and wasted. He looked as if he had not been able to hold food down for days. At that very moment, the chief vomited up what looked like an entire camas bulb. Then his head jerked back . . . and he was dead! I was shocked by the suddenness of it. The Indians around me all began to talk at once. The only word I could make out was *camas*.

Sandy seemed to have a better grasp on what they were saying.

"They're angry with the Cowlitz chief," he whispered. "They think he put a charm on Futillifum when he ate a meal of camas in his village. Though maybe that was a long time ago."

"Do they know that I'm a doctor?" I asked Sandy nervously.

Sandy shook his head. "Even if they did, it wouldn't count with them. They do things differently. I just thought maybe you could help. I was thinking about how you fixed Bo'sun Black's leg."

Futillifum's sudden death had a ripple effect through the entire community. It created a lot of tension among the native people all up and down the river. Doctor McLoughlin decided that the crew had better return to the *William and Ann* before things heated up any more. It gave Douglas less time to get his plants and seeds together to send back to London—and this was no small task. The sixteen bundles that were ready to go took up half his hut, leaving little room to work. It was astonishing how much he had collected in just one summer.

I spent hours sorting out a chest of seeds. Douglas wanted to keep back a few of each kind he had collected in case our ship was lost at sea (a discouraging thought!) or the chest was damaged during the long voyage. The ones I picked out all had to be labeled and repacked so they could be sent east by the overland route in the spring.

Meantime, Douglas had letters to write. He also wanted to make a copy of his journal for Doctor Sabine. Every evening and far into the night, he scribbled away by lamplight, hunched over his makeshift desk, peering nearsightedly at his notebook through his round spectacles.

In spite of all he had to do, he also insisted that Sandy write a letter to his Aunt Agnes.

"But she can't read," the lad protested.

"Your cousin Ronnie can read it—the one who goes to school. Write to him. He can tell the others where you are. Tell him what it's like here."

Douglas bustled about and sat the boy down at his desk. He gave him a sheet of paper.

Sandy stared at the blank page. "I can't do it!" he said, laying down the pen. "I can write the words on labels that you tell me to write—lupine, fir, pinedrop, bear grass—but how can I find words to tell Ronnie and Aunt Agnes what it's like here? How can I tell them that the forest has no end and you can travel on a river for days and weeks before it empties into the sea?"

"Start by writing, 'Dear Ronnie,'" Douglas suggested.

"Why do I have to write *dear*?"

"That's how you always begin a letter! Then tell him you're at Fort Vancouver."

"He won't know where that is," Sandy argued.

"Say it's on the Columbia River, the great river that flows into the Pacific. They'll have a map of the world at school."

"That won't show him how far away we are," Sandy said stubbornly.

"Tell him it took the ship from summer all the way through to the following spring to get here."

In the end it was more Douglas' letter than Sandy's, but the boy seemed to be happy with it when it was finished. "There won't be such a hole in their lives now that they know where

I am," he said. "They'll be able to picture me looking after the pigs. Maybe they can even see me riding in a canoe with the Indians. And Ronnie'll be glad to know I can read."

Douglas was planning to take his bundles and boxes down to the ship himself so that he could see that everything was safely stowed in a dry place in the hold, but he did entrust some of his collection to me when I left with the rest of the crew. Aside from a few warnings on Douglas' side to make sure the plants came to no harm on the trip downriver, we parted quite casually, knowing we would be seeing one another again in a couple of weeks. We could say our farewells then.

Back on the *William and Ann*, it was nice having the cabin to myself, but I found I missed Douglas' company. It was going to be a long trip home. But for now, there was plenty to keep me busy. A great number of shorebirds had gathered at the river's mouth. I just had to mention a bird, and Indians would bring it to me in exchange for an inch or two of tobacco. By this time I had picked up enough of the Chinook jargon to tell them what I needed. Given a few weeks longer, I could have had a specimen of every animal up and down the river.

I was growing impatient for Douglas to show up. I could not match his plant collection, but I was ahead of him on birds! I had my best shorebirds laid out on my bunk, when Captain Hanwell dropped in.

"I just got some more bundles of plants and boxes of seeds from David Douglas," he said. "He wants you to see to them."

"Why can't he see to them himself?" I asked.

"He's still up at the fort. He fell on a rusty nail while he was packing, and now he has an abscessed knee. It's too bad he's not here so that you could take a look at it."

The news worried me. Douglas had to be in bad shape to send his precious collection downriver unsupervised. I could picture his frustration.

But the next news we heard was more encouraging. The abscess was draining. Even though his leg was still stiff and painful, he was planning a collecting trip to Whitbey Harbor on the coast. He hoped to reach the mouth of the Columbia before our ship left.

I sat down and wrote a quick letter to him, pointing out that the bad weather that would make travel difficult was actually on his side. We would not be crossing the bar until the wind dropped, so it might be several days before we sailed. I gave the note to an Indian messenger, hoping he would catch Douglas at Oak Point on the Columbia.

After that, there was nothing to do but wait.

Early on the morning of October 25, the weather eased up and we weighed anchor. Douglas still hadn't come.

I watched the receding shoreline with a heavy heart. It was an uneasy ending to our great adventure. I hated leaving Olla-piska behind without any farewells.

That same evening, Douglas brought his own journal up to date, describing how narrowly we had missed one another, though it was some years before I was privileged to read it.

*Learning the ship had been detained by contrary winds, and finding myself much recovered, I left for Vancouver in a small canoe, with four Indians, for the purpose of visiting my old shipmates on my way to Whitbey Harbour . . . . I camped at the junction of the Multnomah River at sundown, having made only twenty miles, a strong wind setting in from the sea. On Sunday at daylight, I embarked, but before leaving my encampment the canoe had to be fresh gummed. I had not proceeded many miles when it struck on the stump of a tree, which split it from one end to the other, and I had to paddle to shore without loss of time, the water rushing in fast.*

*During the time my Indians were repairing it I occupied the office of cook. I made myself a small basin of tea and boiled some salmon for them. At ten o'clock I proceeded on my route. At eight the same evening, I put ashore at the village of Oak Point to procure some food, where an Indian gave me a letter from Mr. Scouler, the surgeon of the ship, who informed me in his note they would not yet leave for a few days, and as the vessel was seen that same day in the bay I was desirous of writing to Mr. Sabine up to that date. After obtaining a few dried salmon and a wild goose, I went on four miles further down the river, where we took some supper, and continued my journey at ten o'clock, expecting to reach the sea before daylight, being only forty-three miles distant. At four in the morning of Monday a strong westerly breeze set in, which produced a very angry swell on the river and obliged me to cast along the shore . . . .*

*I landed at the mouth of the river at 9 A.M. where I was informed by the Indians the ship had sailed an hour before. I felt no little disappointed, having my letter ready to hand on board. After breakfast my canoe-men lay down to sleep, and I took my gun and knapsack and walked along the bay in quest of some seeds.*

It was typical of David Douglas that he conquered his disappointment by setting off to look for seeds. His interest in the plant kingdom went far beyond that of anyone I have ever known—even our beloved professor, William Hooker. I left the Columbia country with the hope that some day David Douglas and I would be partners in another adventure, but that was not to be.

*Camassia leichtlinii* (large camas)

# *We Call Him Olla-piska*

## by T'Catisa
### Chief Cockqua's Daughter

*The root of the* Phalangium esculentum *[camas] is much used by the natives as a substitute for bread. . . . The Indians have two methods of preparing these roots: they sometimes boil them & eat them cold; but their more favourite method is to compact them into a cake, which they bake by placing it under heated stones & covering them with hot ashes. Baked in this manner they are very palatable.*

Dr. John Scouler's Journal
May 2, 1825

# CHAPTER 10

Even from inside the strong walls of the cedar lodge, I could hear his pain in the howling wind. Mostly I didn't pay much heed to the storms that battered the shore, but that day I couldn't shut out the angry wind. Someone was in trouble. I tried to work on a basket to take my mind off his pain, but the light was poor and the pattern kept going wrong. A bad sign.

Laying my weaving aside, I gave ear to the words of K'atsuk, the storyteller. It was our custom to while away the dark time of the year with stories of our people's past. Old K'atsuk was standing on the other side of the fire pit. From where I sat, I could watch the shadow of her arms moving up and down the wall with the rise and fall of her words. When someone tossed another log on the fire, the sparks flew and K'atsuk's face looked even more wrinkled than usual in the flickering light.

She was telling the story about how the world began. At first there was nothing but sky and fog and water. When the dry land formed, there were only two trees—a redwood to the south and an ash to the north. The trees grew buds that fell to the ground like summer rain. And everywhere the buds landed, grass and flowers sprang up.

Perhaps it was the mention of grass and flowers that brought Olla-piska into my mind. Olla-piska was a white man who had come all the way from King George Land to gather every kind of flower and seed that grows here. He was not like the other white men. All they cared about was the fur of the otter and the beaver. I had seen them take so many beaver skins that I was afraid the day would come when the beaver no longer built their dams across the streams. There would be no meadows where the willow trees grew and the deer browsed. Those white men took the skins without thanking the animal's spirit, and now even some of my own people did not respect the beaver's spirit any more. All they wanted was more and more skins—and then they needed still more so they could buy guns at the fort and shoot even more beaver.

Even before Olla-piska came to our village here on the Cheecheeler River, we had heard about the man who peered at plants through little round glasses. He filled his big tin box with seeds and flowers and squashed them flat between pieces of paper. The rain could soak his clothing and his blanket, and he still kept going. But if the rain touched his plants, he became sad and angry, even though the forests and grasslands were overflowing with more flowers.

The strangest tales were about how he could drink boiling water and light his pipe with fire from the sun. That was how he earned his name—Olla-piska, the man of fire. I thought that he must be happy to have the name my people gave him. It came off the tongue more easily than *David Dug-glass*!

Several moons ago, when I met Olla-piska, I was disappointed. I'd thought he would be a tall man—as tall as White Eagle at the fort. I'd heard that his hair was the color of fire, but it looked more like a fire that was turning to ash! His face was as red as the setting sun, and the skin on his pointed nose was peeling away. But he had a gentle manner and always addressed the spirit of a plant before he picked it. He called every plant by a special name.

On the day Olla-piska came to our village, we were about to feast on a sturgeon that was so big it filled a canoe. My father, Cockqua, chief of the Chinooks, welcomed the King George man to our house, greeting him as *Clachouie*—friend. He told me to fetch water so that Olla-piska could wash. Then he kindled a fire down by the river and asked Olla-piska which part of the fish he wanted cooked for him. Olla-piska quickly replied that Cockqua should choose, which pleased my father. White men are not always so polite.

I knew all too well what was in my father's mind that day. It had always been his goal to marry me off to a King George man. Having a white husband for his youngest daughter would be good security in his old age. A chief's daughter is worth quite a few guns and blankets. My father would surely be able to count on a steady supply of tobacco from the fort to the end of his days.

So when Chief Cockqua honored his guest by giving him the best meat from the head and spine, I was uneasy. It was true that the wives of King George men had a soft life at the fort. All they had to do was take care of their children and sit outside the gate and gossip. There were men to wash the clothes and clean the lodge. But that wasn't the life I wanted.

By the time everyone had eaten their fill of sturgeon, the sun was sinking into the ocean, staining the sky red. My father invited Olla-piska to sleep in our lodge. Clatsop warriors were gathering on the other side of the river, and Olla-piska would be safer inside. But he chose to sleep in his own tent, which he put up about fifty paces outside the village. This raised him up in my father's eyes. He said that Olla-piska was a brave man.

That night, the Clatsops didn't put the white man's bravery to the test. All they did was sing their war songs. So the next morning, my father challenged the plant hunter to show them his hunting skill. First, someone tossed up a small circle of grass and one of our warriors shot an arrow through it while it was still in the air. Then it was Olla-piska's turn to show what he could do. He picked up a stone and hurled it at an eagle perched on a stump at the edge of our clearing. When the eagle rose into the sky, Olla-piska shot it on the wing. Our people were impressed. Then, when someone threw his hat into the air, Olla-piska raised his gun and shot away the crown, leaving only the brim.

"Even the Clatsops cannot shoot like you!" my father shouted in great glee.

I watched from a distance, angry at the way neither of them gave any thought to all the work that had gone into making that hat.

Olla-piska stayed with us for many days. Although I didn't want to marry him, it began to vex me that he never looked my way. My carefully braided hair was black and shiny, and I moved lightly on my feet. Other men noticed me, but not Olla-piska. He called me *tenar*, which means "child" in our speech, or sometimes *chee chee*, "little one." In his own language, he called me *little girl*.

But I was no longer a little girl! A winter and a spring had come and gone since I had become a woman. I had already been on my spirit quest — five days and nights alone among the long grasses by the river. On the last night, I dreamed of the redwing blackbird. He became my guardian spirit. The redwing told me that I would be a basket maker. He also told me that my baskets would travel to places where I would never go.

My pride was hurt by the way Olla-piska paid more heed to my baskets than to the weaver. Didn't he know that the baskets themselves were proof that I was a woman? "Little girls" did not have weaving skills to match mine.

Nor did they make hats for tribal chiefs.

When my father saw that Olla-piska admired his hat, he quickly took it off his head and presented it to the white man, saying, "T'Catisa can easily make more hats. Three? Four?"

Olla-piska turned the hat over in his hand and said it was fine workmanship. He would like to send some back to King George Land. I was happy to think of those faraway people admiring my work, but it stung that Olla-piska only thought of my hats as something to give away.

My father heaped the white man with baskets, reed caps, cups, and pouches. Olla-piska studied them all with great interest. He wanted to know about the plants they were made from and where he could find them.

"T'Catisa will show you the place," my father said eagerly.

I knew that he was picturing Olla-piska following me through the big trees to the marshy place by the river where I always go to gather cattails and sedges. I would be wearing my new cedar-bark skirt that swayed as I walked. I would have red feathers woven into my braids and a circle of the white shells we call dentalia to show off my slender neck.

And that is how it was.

Except that Olla-piska's eyes were always on the ground! When he stopped, it was only to pick a flower or to peer at a mushroom. When he finally spoke, it was only to ask me if I could show him where the camas grew. He'd eaten the bulbs, and he wanted to see what the plants looked like.

"At this time of year, there's nothing to see," I answered sharply. "It is only in the spring that the meadow is blue with flowers."

Olla-piska looked so downcast that when we came to the place where the forest meets the marsh, I showed him the skunk cabbage.

"Our people have a story about this plant," I told him. "In the old days, there were no salmon in our rivers. There was nothing to eat but the leaves and roots of the skunk cabbage. Then the spring salmon came up the river for the first time. A voice from the shore shouted, 'Here come our relatives with their bodies full of eggs.' 'Who speaks to us?' asked the salmon. 'It is your uncle, skunk cabbage,' came the answer. Salmon went ashore to see him. As a reward for having fed the people all these years, salmon gave him an elk-skin blanket and a war club and set him in the rich soil by the river. See how he stands there proudly today in his blanket, holding his war club high!"

I could tell that Olla-piska liked my stories. He seemed to follow them, though he sometimes made me repeat words he didn't know. He worked hard to get their meaning.

When I found some huckleberries that were green, he asked me to come back and pick them for him when they were ripe. He wanted to grow the seeds in King George Land.

"The plants won't be happy there," I said. "These huckleberries belong here in our forests. They don't want to live in another land."

"They'll be well cared for," he said smiling down at me. "People will grow them in their gardens."

"Plants are not like white people," I argued. "They will not be happy in a faraway place."

"Some white people are not happy in this faraway place," Olla-piska answered.

At first, I thought Olla-piska was speaking about himself. But then I found out that he was thinking about someone at the fort. His name was Sandy Ross. "He's not much older than you," Olla-piska said.

The boy ached for the faraway land where he belonged. No

trees grew in the land he came from. He thought that the land here was too dark. He missed the sea and the wide sky. Olla-piska's voice grew quiet when he talked about this boy called Sandy. I felt his sadness for the boy.

Then I heard the call of the redwing blackbird. He flew between us, landing on a nearby willow. My spirit bird was telling me to listen closely to Olla-piska when he talked about this boy. Someday I would know him.

We had been gone from the village for a long time, and I was growing hungry, so I took some camas cakes from my basket and asked Olla-piska if he would like to eat.

"If we had a fire, I could cook them," I offered.

"I can make fire," he answered.

This was what I'd been hoping for!

Olla-piska gathered some withered grass and mounded it on a dry piece of ground. Then he took the little glass that he wore like a necklace and held it so that it caught the fire from the sun. Soon smoke was winding upwards from the grass. He blew on it gently until it was licked by flame. Then he added small sticks, one twig at a time, until the flame was strong. I was happy to have seen Olla-piska's fire magic. When the fire was hot, I placed the camas cakes on a stone and covered them with hot ashes. Olla-piska boiled water for the tea that he said he liked better than food.

While we ate, Olla-piska studied the flowers he had picked. I was tired of being less in his eyes than the deer fern or the honeysuckle. Every girl knows that *tlopit* is a powerful love medicine. So, on our way home, I deliberately led him through the meadow where the *tlopit* bloomed. But even though the petals dusted Olla-piska's clothes, he still didn't see me as I skipped ahead of him through the meadow. His eyes never left the ground. As for me, I was seeing the boy from the land with no trees. I tried to get Olla-piska to tell me more about him, but he would only talk about plants and flowers.

When we got back to the lodge, my father could tell that Olla-piska was not burning up with love. But Cockqua didn't give up. After Olla-piska had gone away, he ordered me to make three more hats.

"He doesn't want to marry me," I protested.

"Of course, he wants you!" my father answered, drawing himself up to his full height. "You are a beautiful young woman. And it would be a good life for you. Think of how White Eagle treats his woman."

I picked up my weaving with a sigh. I could have pointed out that White Eagle had taken his wife far away from her tribe. She came to this land with a heavy heart. She even had to leave some of her own children behind. But I didn't bother to say this, because I knew I would never marry Olla-piska. He didn't look at me the way a man looks at a woman he wants.

Nevertheless, when the hats were finished, my father confidently set off toward the rising sun in search of Olla-piska. It wouldn't be hard to find the plant hunter. Our people always knew his whereabouts. But when my father came back, he didn't bring the promise of a husband for his daughter—only a blanket for himself and some needles, beads, pins, and rings as a present for the "little girl."

While my thoughts had been wandering through the meadows with Olla-piska, K'atsuk had come to the end of her story. Her last words hung in the air. "And since then there has always been trouble in the world."

The wind howled sadly in the treetops.

"Trouble . . . and pain!" I whispered. "Someone out there is in pain!"

The words slipped out of my mouth and seemed to fill the room.

Everyone turned and stared at me.

"Is it someone known to us?"

I nodded.

For now I knew whose pain I had been feeling during the storm. It was Olla-piska's pain—the man who talked to plants. That was why he had filled my thoughts all evening.

# CHAPTER 11

*Chief Cockqua's Village*
*November 1825*

The door suddenly burst open, filling the lodge with the noise of the storm. Tha-a-muxi stumbled in. He was a chief from one of the villages farther up the Cheecheeler River. Usually, Tha-a-muxi filled any room he entered with noise and laughter, but today he was too weary even to greet us. Two other men followed. They half-carried a sagging figure between them. From his clothes, everyone could tell that he was a King George man. When the two men let go of him, he slumped to the floor like a discarded cloak.

"It's Olla-piska!" K'atsuk exclaimed. Olla-piska, the man of fire — but his fire was nearly out.

"Why do you bring him here?" one of the elders asked Tha-a-muxi. There was a sharp edge to his voice as he added, "We don't want him."

It wouldn't go well if anything happened to Olla-piska while he was under our roof. White Eagle had sent out a message that our people were to help David Douglas find all the plants and seeds he needed. While he traveled in our land, he was under White Eagle's cloak. Nothing must befall him.

"We were trying to reach my village," Tha-a-muxi answered. "But we have not had a full stomach in many days, and Olla-piska has poison in his leg. He can go no farther."

Some of the women quickly got a meal together — dried salmon, huckleberries, and camas root. Olla-piska ate next to nothing. He crouched close to the fire, warming his shaking hands.

When the food was gone, everyone gathered around Tha-a-muxi to hear the story of his travels. Olla-piska had wanted to see his friends on the winged ship before it sailed back to King George Land, but he was late in starting out from Fort Vancouver because of the poison in his leg. When he reached the shore, the wind was already carrying the ship out to sea. He missed seeing his friends by the blink of an eye. So he came to the lodge of Tha-a-muxi's brother, Chief Madsu, hoping to find someone to guide him to the Cheecheeler River, which lay to the north and was where he wanted to go next. Tha-a-muxi was visiting his brother.

"He wants to find the seeds of the *somuchtan* – the plant he calls lupine – that grows near our river," Tha-a-muxi explained. "When he learned that my village is on the banks of the Cheecheeler, he asked me to take him there. I said my canoe was too small. My brother said he would lend us one of his big canoes. With it, we could travel on the ocean. Some of his people would go with us to bring the canoe back."

"Where are Chief Madsu's people now?" K'atsuk asked.

One of the other men took up the story.

"Olla-piska was anxious to set out for the Cheecheeler, but we had not gone far before the pain came back to his knee. Maybe the journey was too hard. To reach the place where the stream runs north into Willapa Bay, we had to carry Chief Madsu's big canoe over rocks and stumps and drag it across gullies. When we reached the bay, we slept under a shelf of rock above the tide mark. The rains blew in and soaked us, and the sea was so angry that we had to move our blankets two times in the night to escape the waves."

The next day, they had traveled up the coast. But the big canoe was no match for the storm, and most of their food washed overboard. All they had left was a few kinnikinnick berries and some arrowhead roots. The wind battered the boat, and the rain was so heavy that when they put ashore they couldn't get a fire going. The village where they'd hoped to get dried salmon was deserted. They were afraid to chance the ocean again in such a storm, but carrying the heavy canoe overland would be impossible. Finally, Tha-a-muxi told Madsu's men to take the canoe back to their chief. He and Olla-piska and the two men from his village would find their way through the forest to the Cheecheeler River.

The storm had driven all the seabirds far inland, so the men traveled on empty stomachs. They spent the dark hours hunched together in small shelters woven from pine branches. Yesterday, they finally had some good luck. At dusk, Olla-piska limped out with his gun and brought down five ducks with one shot! Tha-a-muxi and his two men were so hungry they didn't take time to pluck the birds. They singed off the feathers and ate them only partly cooked. But Olla-piska had no appetite and made do with a basin of tea. After that, they all slept.

Without a canoe, they couldn't go up the Cheecheeler River to reach Tha-a-muxi's village. They had to bring Olla-piska to Cockqua's lodge.

My father, who had kept his silence throughout the story, now turned and addressed Olla-piska. "We are happy that you are honoring us with another visit, *Clachouie*," he said.

Olla-piska's voice was so weak that his answer was lost.

After a long silence, my father spoke again.

"T'Catisa will look at your leg," he said. "She is skilled in every healing medicine. She can make your leg well."

I couldn't believe the words coming from my father's mouth! I threw a begging look toward K'atsuk. The old woman had far more healing wisdom than I did. The little that I knew I had learned from her. She should be the one to treat the poison in Olla-piska's leg.

But K'atsuk refused to catch my eye. She wasn't going to go against the wishes of Chief Cockqua. If he wanted his daughter to practice her healing on the white man, that was how it should be. Moreover, why should she take the risk of treating a man who sheltered under White Eagle's cloak? The price of failure would be much too high.

I knew all too well why my father was making such a foolish boast. Once again, he was trying to get Olla-piska to notice me. But this time, if I failed, it wouldn't only be my pride that was hurt. White Eagle didn't care about the outcome of our dealings with each other, but he would not forgive our village if I gave bad medicine to his friend.

"Let T'Catisa look at your knee," my father repeated.

Everyone stepped back so that I could kneel down beside the sick man. He smiled at me weakly and said, "The little basket maker!"

It was a good sign that he knew me in spite of his pain. Rolling up the leg of his trousers, I looked at his knee and touched the wound with gentle fingers. It was an angry purple color, with streaks of deep red running away from it. The only thing in my medicine pouch that might draw out the poison was the leaves of the *t'sit'sialkum*. When I showed the dried leaves to Olla-piska, he called them yellow avens. He knew the plant even when its color was gone.

"I'll gladly try your medicine," he told me quietly. "But let *me* put the poultice on my leg after you have prepared it. Then I'll bleed myself to bring down the fever. "

I felt a wave of relief. Olla-piska knew the risk I had been asked to take. That was why he chose to put the medicine on the leg himself. Knowing this, I also knew that I could love this man. I no longer cared that he was old and that his hair was thin. I no longer minded that he peered at the world through glass eyes. I loved him because he was gentle and I would be safe sleeping under his blanket.

That night, I had a strange dream. I saw Olla-piska walking along a trail with a small dog at his heels. The trail suddenly fell away. The dog stopped, but Olla-piska kept on walking. I woke up with a start. I was relieved to see Olla-piska sleeping peacefully on a platform near the fire. And when morning came, the wound was so much better that he could stand again.

The leg healed quickly. The medicine had worked!

But Olla-piska did not look at me through new eyes. He hardly looked at me at all. He just wanted to be off searching for the seeds of the *somuchtan*.

During the days that Olla-piska stayed with us, he asked everyone who visited about a tree with huge cones that hold sweet seeds. He had met some people who carried the seeds in their tobacco pouches and ate them like nuts. They were hard to come by because the sugar pine tree that bears the sweet seeds does not live here. It grows far to the south, in the land of the Umpquas. Whenever Olla-piska spoke of the giant cones, his voice was filled with longing. But my father and several of the elders all warned him not go south. Both the land and the people held too many dangers.

Olla-piska didn't hear them, and I knew he wouldn't rest till he held the cones in his hand. The tree was calling him. This was his spirit quest. There could be no turning away.

With his leg healed and his *somuchtan* seeds safely in his tin box, Olla-piska was ready to move on. He was going to paddle up the Cheecheeler in a borrowed canoe to Tha-a-muxi's village. Then he would go back to White Eagle's fort by land.

As my father watched him leave, I think he knew that this King George man would never be his daughter's husband. I knew it, too, and I felt sad. That night, I dreamed about Olla-piska and his little dog again. He was walking along the trail that suddenly dropped away.

*Lupinus sulphureus kincaidii* (Kincaid's lupine)

# The Sugar Pine Quest

## by David Douglas
Botanist and Explorer

*I rejoice to tell you of a new species of Pinus, the most princely of the genus, perhaps even the grandest specimen of vegetation. It attains the enormous height of one hundred and seventy to two hundred and twenty feet, with a circumference of fifty feet, and cones from twelve to eighteen inches long! . . . This Pinus is found abundantly two degrees south of the Columbia River, in the country of the Umpqua tribe of Indians.*

> from a letter to William Hooker from
> David Douglas
> March 24, 1826

*Last night was one of the most dreadful I ever witnessed. . . . Sleep of course was not to be had, every ten or fifteen minutes immense trees falling producing a crash as if the earth was cleaving asunder. . . . My poor horses were unable to endure the violence of the storm without craving of me protection, which they did by hanging their heads over me and neighing.*

> David Douglas' Journal
> October 25, 1826

# CHAPTER 12

*The Umpqua Valley*
*September to October 1826*

On returning from the Cheecheeler River in 1825, my mood was as dark as the heavy, gray November sky. Collecting had gone badly because of the stormy weather and my abscessed knee. The only bright spot was the way the Indians took care of me — especially T'Catisa, Cockqua's young daughter.

Another reason for gloom was that when the Hudson's Bay Express arrived from the east with the mail, it brought nothing from England. The ship with the English mail had been late in reaching York Factory on Hudson's Bay, and the Express hadn't waited for it. That meant it would be another year before any mail on board could be delivered. Another year without any words of encouragement from Doctor Hooker. Another year without news of my family.

There was, however, a bright side to mail that traveled no faster than a man could carry it. In the spring I'd written to Doctor Sabine asking for permission to stay longer in the Northwest. Instead of boarding the *Dryad* at the mouth of the Columbia in the autumn, I proposed traveling with the Express to York Factory, where I'd catch a ship bound for England. This would give me more time to devote to my collection and save me the tedious voyage around the Cape. Knowing that Doctor Sabine's reply couldn't reach me before the *Dryad* sailed, I was free to stay, no matter what he answered!

I meant to put my extra time in the Northwest to good use. The sugar pine beckoned. I had written to Professor Hooker, telling him about the cone that Jean Baptiste McKay had shown me, and my collection wouldn't be complete without one. But Doctor McLoughlin kept insisting that I mustn't go to the Umpqua on my own. He warned me that it was rugged country and the Indians were unfriendly.

The cones were on my mind all summer. Then, in September 1826, fortune smiled. When I returned to Fort Vancouver from a collecting trip upcountry to the Snake River, Doctor McLoughlin greeted me with the news that Alexander McLeod had just left for the Umpqua, leading a brigade.

"If you start tomorrow, you could easily catch up with them," he said "It's a large group with extra horses, so they won't be traveling fast. I'll give you my mare. She's a steady animal."

It was typical of Doctor McLoughlin to offer me his own horse. Throughout my stay at the fort, I was touched by his generosity and his concern for my safety.

Without stopping to sort out the specimens from my summer trip, I started making preparations. While I was checking out my gear, Sandy dropped in to welcome me back. He scowled when he heard that I was leaving again. I explained that it was my only chance to see the sugar pines and then tried to cheer him by showing him my new gun.

My old one was no longer reliable, and I needed to shoot game while I was traveling. "It cost two pounds at the trading post," I told Sandy. "I'm going to get a grizzly skin! And I bought a new copper kettle." I counted off the items laid out on my bunk. "One strong linen shirt and one flannel shirt; some beads, rings, and trinkets for presents; tobacco for trading. I'm taking two blankets as well as my tent. Doctor McLoughlin says we're bound to run into bad weather at this time of year."

"And this?" Sandy asked, pointing to a bulky package.

"You know fine what that is!" I answered. "Six quires of paper for pressing flowers. It's heavy, but I can't make do with less."

"I could go along and carry it," Sandy volunteered hopefully.

He'd have been good company, and I was proud of the way he'd picked up the names of so many plants, but Doctor

McLoughlin would never let him go. With so many of the men away, he needed all hands to help with the harvest. Besides, it was going to be a long, hard journey.

"When we get back, I'll see if you can be spared for a couple of weeks to go to the coast to visit my friend Cockqua," I promised. "I want to show you where the lupines grow so that you can collect seeds for me next summer."

Sandy was scowling again. Seeing where the lupines grow was no substitute for traveling with the brigade into Indian country. As it turned out, both trips would have their dismal moments.

I was off before daybreak and caught up with the brigade around four o'clock in the afternoon at a camping place about fifty miles up the Willamette River. Mister McLeod greeted me warmly. Even though the camp had a settled look with Indians and trappers and their wives working about the place and children running everywhere, he assured me we'd break camp the next day.

It was a chilly evening, so after I'd pitched my tent, I joined a group of men sitting around a blazing fire. A huge chunk of meat sizzled over the flames. Roasted venison and a basin of tea! What more could I ask for? The western sky glowed red with the setting sun. A good omen, I thought. I was at peace with the world.

My mood turned to impatience the next morning when I learned that several horses had strayed into the forest, so we couldn't set off as planned. It took three days to round them up. The bright side was that I had more than enough time to look at every plant and seedpod along the riverbank. I reminded myself that the sugar pines had been growing for hundreds of years—a few days' wait wouldn't matter. All the same, I wished I could press on alone. I wasn't used to matching the pace of a brigade.

At long last, the straggling procession was on its way, heading west toward the coast through gently rolling country dotted with pines and solitary oaks. It would have been like riding through a magnificent parkland, except that the whole countryside was burned black and the horses found the charred ground difficult. After about two hours, we stopped by a stream where a few clumps of grass were growing along the banks. We'd only covered about five miles, but the horses were hungry and thirsty.

I presumed that the fire had been started by a lightning strike, but one of the Indians told me that it was deliberately set to make hunting easier by forcing the deer into the unburned areas. Another Indian said the land was burned over so they could find wild honey and grasshoppers for winter food. Whatever the reason, there was little in the charred landscape of interest to a botanist.

The following day dawned clear and fine with a westerly wind. We were moving by nine, this time heading due south. Most of the country was still burned black with only small patches of green in the valleys. The burned stumps and brushwood hurt my feet, but I wanted to spare McLoughlin's mare any extra weight.

The next day was Sunday. We covered eighteen miles before setting up camp on the banks of a small stream that flowed into the Willamette River, three miles to the east. Sundays were like any other day — we walked till we were weary, set up camp, and then went out hunting for our supper. The only differences were that we changed our shirts and those men who knew how to read studied their Bibles in the evening.

After supper, I went hunting with John Kennedy, a jovial Irishman with flaming red hair and a bushy beard of the same color. We hadn't gone far when we spotted a big wasp nest lying on the bare ground.

"It was likely left by bears," Kennedy observed.

The words were scarcely out of his mouth when a huge grizzly lumbered out of the brush about two hundred yards ahead of us. Remembering my boast to Sandy, I thought about going after it, but it was growing dark so I left the beast in peace.

A few days later, who should we meet up with but Jean Baptiste McKay! He and his two Indian hunters were on their way north from the Umpqua, but seeing they had no fixed plan, they decided to join us and head south again.

"So you're still stalking the big cones!" he said. "I had one of my hunters go after them a few days ago, but he lost the scent! We got us a grizzly instead!"

When he showed me the skin, I asked how much he wanted for it. We settled on a blanket and some tobacco as a fair trade. I was pleased with the deal. The nights were cold, and the skin would made a good warm ground cover.

A day later, John Kennedy nearly lost *his* skin to a grizzly. Afterward we joked about it, saying that the bear had fancied his red pelt and must have been disgruntled only to get his trousers, but it wasn't funny at the time. Kennedy didn't see the creature until he was within a few yards of it, and then his gun misfired. No one can outrun a bear, so Kennedy scrambled up into a small oak tree. The animal was close enough to grab him—one paw on his back and the other under his right arm. Luckily, his coat and trousers were so old and threadbare that they ripped away, or that would have been the last of John Kennedy.

We were fortunate that Baptiste McKay decided to throw his lot in with us. In addition to being a great hunter and storyteller, he had a flair for cooking. One memorable morning, he fixed a magnificent breakfast for McLeod and me—roasted shoulder of doe and mint tea sweetened with a little sugar. He served the meat on glossy leaves of salal and the tea in a large dish hewn out of solid wood. We supped with spoons made from the horns of mountain sheep. After we shared a pipe with a few Indians from the Umpqua tribe, we packed up and followed the rugged track along the banks of a small stream. By this time, I had settled into the rhythm of traveling with the brigade.

The burned-over land was far behind us, but traveling was no easier. We were now leading the horses and had to fight every step of the way through the forest. McLeod and I went ahead, followed by McKay and his two hunters, chopping off branches that hindered the horses' progress. It was weary work. There was never more than a hundred yards of level ground, and our way was often blocked by fallen trees, some of them eight feet in diameter and as much as two hundred and fifty feet long. I took notes when I wasn't swinging a hatchet. And I kept adding treasures to my vasculum—brightly colored mushrooms, creeping liverworts, and mosses of every kind. I wished Scouler was with me to share in the excitement of these finds.

The footing was so bad for the horses that I didn't trust my plant press to my mare. Instead, I carried it on my own back, tied up in a hide. It made a cumbersome load, but that didn't stop me from adding to it. I couldn't pass up a shed horn of a black-tailed deer, and I tied that to my bundle, too. McKay claimed that, from behind, I looked like some strange, mismatched animal.

Our first sight of the Umpqua River was one of the great moments of the trip. From the summit of the last ridge, we gazed down on the silver river winding through the green valley far below. McLeod and I let out a wild cheer and slid straight down the steep mountainside.

Our route was too steep for the men leading the horses, and most of them had a hard time finding a safe way down. My horse was among the laggards. It was long past dinnertime, and it still hadn't showed up. I couldn't go to bed because my blanket and bearskin robe were on the horse's back, so I spent the evening drying out my seeds and transferring plants to fresh paper. Then I settled down to spend the night by the fire with only my plant press for company.

Around two o'clock, McLeod came over and joined me.

"Let me take your place by the fire for a while," he whispered. "I'll be warm enough in this greatcoat. You can have my blanket and buffalo robe."

Touched by his generosity, I spent the rest of the night in relative comfort.

The last of the men and horses straggled into the camp about four o'clock the following afternoon. When I saw the way the tin box that held my notebooks was bent out of shape, I was glad I'd carried the plant press on my back. A small case of preserving powder was spoiled, and my spare shirt was so rubbed that it was like a piece of surgeon's lint.

McLeod decided to set up a base camp by the Umpqua so that he could rest the horses for a while before going farther south. This suited me well. According to McKay, we were within a few days journey of the sugar pine trees. He offered me one of his Indian hunters as a guide.

"He knows the area," he told me. "We came through the mountain range where the big trees grow on our way north. He speaks some Chinook and understands the Umpqua tongue, so you'll be safe with him."

The Indian was a handsome youth, about sixteen or seventeen years old.

"What tribe is he from?" I asked McKay.

"I don't know . . . and neither does he. He was captured by a war party in the south when he was just a small child. They kept him as a slave till I took him. He likes our way of life and shows no interest in trying to find his own people."

Confident that I was in good hands, we set off on horseback at dawn the next day, following deer trails through the woods. Around mid-morning, we came on two Indian lodges. About twenty-five people — mostly women — poured out to greet us.

"Ask where we can cross the river," I told my young guide.

He looked confused and said nothing, but the women had plenty to say. McKay had apparently overrated the lad's language skills. He couldn't understand what I wanted him to ask, and he had no idea what the women were telling us, except that they kept referring to Chief Centrenose. I finally got across that we were hungry and would trade tobacco for food. They brought out a few hazelnuts and camas roots. I'd been hoping for enough food to last us for several days so we wouldn't have to waste time hunting. A little farther along the trail I had the good luck to bring down a small deer.

We eventually gave up looking for a place to ford the river. Instead, I set about making a raft by cutting branches and binding them together, while the lad skinned the deer. After working all day, my hands were rubbed raw, and I had to face it that the raft was too flimsy to withstand the force of the river.

The next morning, my hands were so sore I couldn't swing my hatchet. But we still had to cross the river. Staying on this side would take us out of our way. I scribbled a note to McLeod, asking if he could please spare someone to help me finish the raft.

"Here! Take this to McKay's camp," I said, handing the note to my guide. "Give it to Chief McLeod."

The young Indian had no trouble understanding that I wanted him to head back to camp! He grabbed the note and disappeared down the trail at a run.

Deciding that the day wouldn't be wasted if I could lay in a supply of meat, I bandaged my blistered hands with my kerchief, tethered my horse to a tree, and picked up my gun. Luck was with me. I hadn't gone far into the forest when I got off a shot at a large buck — and that was as far as my luck went. The deer was wounded, but it didn't fall. I plunged after it into the brush. I had only gone a few steps when, without warning, the ground suddenly gave way, and I crashed into a deep gully in a hail of rattling stones and breaking branches. I lay there for some time, swimming in and out of consciousness.

The next thing I knew, five Indians were peering down at me. They'd apparently found my horse and tracked me down by my muffled groans. After easing me out of the gully, they laid me on a blanket. I tried to struggle to my feet, but could do no more than sit up. The pain was fierce. Every breath tore at my chest. I peered at my watch and was amazed to find that four hours had passed. I wondered, dizzily, if the hour hand had been pushed forward by the fall.

My only coherent thought was that I needed to get back to the base camp. Two of the Indians eased me to my feet. We formed ourselves into a slow procession, with the Indians leading the horse and me hobbling along with the aid of a stick and my gun. Part way back to camp, we were met by John Kennedy, who was on his way to help me build the raft. The Indians tried to leave when they saw him, but I managed to detain them long enough to convince them to accept the deer I'd shot the day before in payment for their kindness.

"It seems that more than blistered hands ails you, lad!" Kennedy said, looking me up and down. "Let's hoist you onto your horse."

"I can't get up there," I protested.

"You're going to have to, or we'll not make it back before dark," he pointed out. So he had his way.

After what seemed like an eternity, we reached the camp. All I wanted was a basin of strong tea. My ribs ached, and I was shivering even though my brow was clammy with sweat. Scouler might have known what to do about that pain in my chest, but he was far away—no doubt enjoying the comforts of life back in Scotland.

At least I knew how to relieve a fever without his help. I took out my knife and made a cut in my left foot. Bleeding seemed to ease the pain in my chest as well, but it did nothing for the heaviness of my mood. My dream of bringing back a cone from the sugar pine was seeping away like the blood dripping into the dark earth.

# CHAPTER 13

*The Umpqua Valley*
*October to November 1826*

It was a week before I recovered my spirits. My bruised ribs still hurt, but not enough to make me hesitate when Chief Centrenose said that one of his many sons could take me to the mountains where the sugar pines grew. Centrenose himself was going to lead McLeod down the coast, along with half of the brigade. McKay would take the other half due south.

I set off right away, accompanied by the chief's son, who was also named Centrenose. When we reached the place of my earlier troubles, he stopped and kindled a small fire on the riverbank, crouching over it and stoking it with wet wood. I paced up and down, frowning impatiently. We'd hardly finished breakfast, and I wasn't hungry. Besides, there wasn't enough heat in his smoky fire to bring a kettle through the boil. Less than fifteen minutes later, two Indians from upriver showed up in their canoes to check out the smoke.

Now I saw the reason for the fire!

In exchange for some venison, tobacco, beads, and rings, the Indians agreed to ferry us across the rushing river.

I was just beginning to feel confident that this time I'd reach my goal, when the weather turned against us. By mid-afternoon of the next day, the rain was so heavy that I felt as if we were trapped under a waterfall. We could have been walking through a forest of sugar pines, and I wouldn't have known them.

Around five o'clock, the rain let up a little. We were in a small clearing with grass for the horses, so we decided to stop for the night. We finished off the last of the deer meat and — with difficulty — boiled a few ounces of rice.

By now the wind had picked up.

Centrenose wrapped himself in his blanket and lay down near the banked fire, even though there was no way the fire could last through the night. By the time I'd pitched my tent and crawled in, the rain was coming down in torrents and the wind was blowing with what seemed like hurricane force. The snapping canvas and creaking branches took me back to the journey around the Horn.

I eventually drifted off into an uneasy sleep but was rudely awakened when the tent collapsed about my ears. I lay there, rolled in a wet blanket with the drenched canvas piled on top of me, unable to do anything except wish for daylight.

The roaring wind filled the darkness with one long, continuous sound. Trees crashed all around us, and the rumble of thunder and vivid flashes of forked lightning reduced me to a state beyond fear. The poor horses cowered close by, neighing plaintively and hanging their heads over the miserable heap of tent and blankets.

The storm blew itself out toward daylight. By the time the sun was up, the sky had cleared, although it was now bitterly cold. I untangled myself from my sodden wrappings and stood up stiffly, looking around at the damage. Even if Centrenose and I had had a common language, we couldn't have found words to describe the awfulness of the night.

"Lucky miss," I finally said, pointing to a fallen tree that dissected the clearing.

"Lucky miss," Centrenose repeated, shaking his head.

We lit a fire to thaw out our stiff muscles and dry off our clothes. My energy was nearly spent. I *had* to find the cones that day. My best hope was to head out on my own, leaving Centrenose at the storm-strewn campsite with the horses.

Out of habit, before I left I showed him how to dry out my plant papers — it was just a case of separating the sheets and holding them up near the fire — though nothing really mattered now except finding the sugar pine. I could lose my entire collection and still be happy if I could bring back one giant cone heavy with seeds.

After I'd been walking for about an hour, I met a lone Indian. The moment he saw me, he strung his bow, placed a sleeve of raccoon skin on his left arm, and blocked my way. Even though he looked ready to shoot, I was convinced that he was more frightened than anything else. Maybe he'd never seen a white man before. I stood still and laid my gun at my feet, beckoning him to come closer. He hesitated and then inched forward. I gestured to him to place his bow and quiver of arrows beside my gun. Then I lit my pipe and offered him tobacco. While we smoked, I showed him some beads.

"Here! Yours!" I said.

When I could see that he was relaxed, I took my notebook from my pack and drew a rough sketch of a sugar pine tree and a cone. The man watched intently. Suddenly his face lit up. He knew what I wanted! He pointed to a ridge of hills that lay some miles to the south.

"I want to go there," I told him, using my fingers to demonstrate the idea of walking.

The young Indian nodded and smiled.

When I started out, he fell into step beside me.


The stand of sugar pines was even more magnificent than I had imagined. The trunks grew straight up, with no side branches for about two thirds of their height. The bark was smooth and pale, with occasional blisters of bright amber gum. For a long time, I stood at the base of one of the tallest pines—truly the prince of trees—staring up at the huge cones hanging from the points of its blue-green branches. The cones made me think of sugar loaves in a grocer's shop.

But now I had another worry. How could I reach them? There was no way to climb the smooth trunk—or to hack through it. The only thing to do—and this was something I'd often done before—was to shoot the cones out of the tree.

But first I felt a frantic need to write everything down. I wanted to describe the tree for people in England in case I didn't live to tell them about it. Even at the time, I knew this didn't make much sense. If I failed to make it back from this adventure, the chances were that my notebook wouldn't either.

I paced out the length of a tree that had been blown down

in an earlier storm—two hundred and fifteen feet! The trunk measured fifty-seven feet and nine inches around.

Then I went back to the tallest standing tree, raised my gun and took careful aim.

To my surprise—and horror—the blast produced more than a shower of twigs and cones. Within moments, I was surrounded by eight Indians. They were armed with bows and arrows, bone-tipped spears, and flint knives. Their faces and bodies were painted with red earth.

I looked all around for my friendly Indian. He had vanished without a trace, leaving me in a bad fix. I needed him to explain that all I wanted was a few pine cones. Pointing to the ones I'd brought down, I tried to tell the Indians that I was willing to trade beads and tobacco for more cones.

At first, they seemed satisfied with my pantomimed explanation. They talked a little among themselves, and then sat down to smoke. But soon one of them began to string his bow, while another sharpened his flint knife and suspended it on the wrist of his right hand. I didn't need any more clues as to what was going to happen next.

Running away was out of the question. Instead, I stepped back about five paces, cocked my gun, and drew a pistol from my belt. With the pistol in my left hand and the gun in my right hand, I made it clear that I was ready to fight for my life.

We stared at each other, nobody making a move or saying a word for what could have been five minutes. It seemed an eternity. Then one of the Indians—I think he was the leader—signed that he wanted tobacco. I signed that they could have it, but first they must bring me more cones.

The Indians set off at once.

As soon as they were out of sight, I snatched up a few twigs and the three cones I'd blasted out of the tree and took off running. Every now and then, I stopped to listen, expecting to hear the sounds of pursuit. All I could hear was my own rasping breath.

When I reached the campsite, I found that Centrenose had restored some order. He proudly showed me the papers he'd dried. Once again we didn't have enough words for me to tell him about my adventures, so I held out my treasured cones. They were all of a size, and they all contained fine seed. The biggest measured fourteen and a half inches long; the smallest, thirteen and a half inches.

Although I was exhausted, I had trouble settling down for the night. My stomach was empty and I jumped at the slightest sound, worried that the Indians had found our camp. I brought my journal up to date by the light of a Columbia candle—a lighted piece of rosiny pine. Then I dropped off into a restless sleep.

An hour or two before dawn, I was startled by a loud shriek. It turned out to be Centrenose. He, too, had gone supperless to bed and had decided to go out in search of trout for breakfast. I crawled out of the tent to find him jumping about, wildly clawing the air.

"Grizzly bear?" I asked.

"Grizzly!" he repeated, drawing his nails down my arm.

"It came after you?"

He nodded.

"I'll shoot it when it's light," I promised. It would be asking for trouble to go after the beast in the dark.

As it turned out, the bear chose the time for the encounter. Before dawn, she lumbered into the campsite with her two cubs. Centrenose and I decided we'd best leave—fast. We stuffed everything into the saddlebags and led the horses some distance away. Then I mounted my mare and rode back into the campsite. McLoughlin had told me she stood fire well.

The mother bear and her cubs were under a big oak tree feeding on acorns. I let the horse walk within twenty yards of them. All three bears stood up and growled. I leveled my gun at the heart of the old one. She tried to protect her young by keeping them right under her, but my first shot hit one of cubs. It fell instantly. A second shot hit the mother on the chest as she stood up with her remaining cub under her belly. She turned and fled into the forest. The wound must have been mortal, because mother bears never leave their cubs unless they themselves are dying. I didn't try to follow her.

Centrenose was happy to get the carcass of the small bear. My three cones were all the trophies I needed.

When we stumbled into the base camp, we found it deserted except for a young Indian lad and Michel La Framboise, a French Canadian *voyageur*. La Framboise had been left in charge of some horses and stores and was overjoyed to see us. He pulled me down from my horse and wrung my hand. He'd been worrying that Indians were planning to take over our near-empty camp.

The following day, a disturbing incident added to our nervousness. An Indian, who had offered to guide two hunters to a small lake about twenty miles away, came into camp wearing a coat and carrying a gun that had belonged to one of the hunters. It looked suspicious. But with unfriendly Indians about and not knowing his language, we didn't dare confront him. We only hoped that the men had been robbed and not murdered. If only the brigade would come back!

When McKay finally showed up, he reported that he, too, had encountered Indian troubles. Over by the coast, one of his men was shot in the heart by an arrow, and an Indian woman — the wife of one of his hunters — was kidnapped along with her five children. I felt lucky to have returned safely to camp.

The next day, McLeod straggled in with the rest of the brigade. On hearing that I'd succeeded in bringing back three giant sugar pine cones, he immediately asked what I wanted to do next.

"I'd like to head back straight back to Fort Vancouver," I told him. "I'm going to be leaving in March with the Express, and I have specimens from my Snake River trip to sort and pack."

"I'm sending a dispatch up to the fort with Kennedy and Fannaux," McLeod said. "If it suits you, you can go along, too. They're leaving right away. There's no point in waiting for better weather this late in the season."

It didn't promise to be a fast trip. We were to take nine horses back to the fort, and we'd have to stop to hunt along the way because McLeod couldn't spare us even basic rations.

Game wasn't easy to find. We traveled for four days without shooting a bird or a deer. On the fifth day, after covering thirty-three miles, drenched with rain, bleached with sleet, and chilled with the piercing north wind, we settled down for the night without supper or a fire.

I was on edge.

"I'm sure we're several miles out of our way," I muttered.

"We're on the route we followed on the way down," Kennedy said sharply.

In the morning, we agreed to head for a small lake that Kennedy thought lay some seven miles to the north. He said it offered our best hope for finding wild fowl. I volunteered to go ahead on foot, leaving the others to bring the horses. The plan was for me to reach the lake by midday and shoot some birds for supper.

About three miles out, I began to wonder if I was heading in the right direction. I decided to retrace my steps and check with the others. It turned out they'd already left. It should have been easy to pick up the trail of nine horses, but I must have been a bit lightheaded from hunger. I couldn't pick up any trace of them. Soon I was totally disoriented, but then I blundered on an old campsite that struck a chord. It was where I'd traded with McKay for the grizzly skin on the way south!

Now I was sure I knew my way to the lake.

My confidence was given a further boost when I brought down three geese and a duck. Close to the lake, I saw a large flock of geese a little to the left of the trail. I set down my hat and the birds I'd already shot and crept toward them.

I only managed to shoot one bird.

Then, when I went back to pick up my belongings, I could find no trace of them. I went over the same ground again and again, but I finally had to give up.

I'd lost four birds for the sake of one!

By now, it was pitch dark, and I had no idea where I was. Then a gunshot rang out, followed by others at regular intervals. I headed toward the sound. Kennedy was bringing me in.

I was almost there, when a cloud of ducks flew right over my head. I fired off a random shot. To my surprise, I hit one, so now I had a duck as well as the goose to bring home for supper!

Kennedy greeted me with mock civility when I stumbled in. "Be seated by the fire, Sire!" he said.

Fannaux plucked the birds and roasted them over the flame, while I warmed my hands on a mug of tea and told them about the mishaps of the day. I didn't mention my aching ribs. I didn't tell them about the throbbing pain behind my eyes. Getting lost in the forest—even losing everyone's supper—was forgivable. But you never complained. In the eyes of a *voyageur,* there was no worse crime.

When we reached the Santiam River, the Indian village where we'd hoped to get canoes was deserted. Fannaux and Kennedy decided to swim their horses across the rain-swollen river. But after seeing Fannaux take a spill midstream, I thought I'd do better striking out on my own without a horse. Luckily, Fannaux had freed himself from the stirrups and managed to swim the rest of the way. The horse made it, too. And I reached the other side safely. My clothing and bedding were soaked and, even worse, my collection was ruined. Putting his own life in jeopardy, Fannaux tried to snatch up a some papers as they floated off down the river and missed. But my three giant cones were unharmed, and that was what I cared about most.

Four days later, we limped into Fort Vancouver.

The hardships of the trip were soon forgotten when I discovered that there were letters waiting for me. As I read and re-read a letter from brother John, I pictured the cottage back in Scone. Suddenly, I couldn't wait to see my family. I could almost hear the fat sizzle and smell the onions cooking as my mother stirred a pot of skirlie over the open fire.

There was also a long letter from Doctor Hooker. I pictured myself handing the professor a sugar-pine cone and describing the splendid tree with its straight trunk and blue-green foliage.

*Yes.* I was ready to go home!

But first there was the promised trip to Chief Cockqua's village with Sandy. When I explained to Doctor McLoughlin that I wanted to show the boy where the wild lupines grow near the coast so that he could collect seeds for me next summer, he gave the trip his blessing and even lent us a small canoe.

November is not a good time to travel in an open boat. When we finally reached the longhouse, the silence was like a gift because our ears had been bombarded for so long by pounding waves and howling gales. Cockqua, looking much the same as last time, stepped forward to greet us.

"Olla-piska!" he exclaimed.

I introduced Sandy.

*"Kloshe tumtum!"* Cockqua greeted him as a friend.

After we'd been given a welcoming meal of dried salmon and camas bulbs, we gathered around the fire and listened to K'atsuk, the storyteller.

Sandy sat very still. But he wasn't listening the story. His eyes never left T'Catisa, Chief Cockqua's daughter.

When night came, I spread my blanket on the lodge floor.

"What about the fleas?" Sandy whispered.

"Maybe I'm growing old, but tonight I'm so glad to have stout walls to keep out the wind that I'll take a chance on the fleas!" I told him.

As it turned out, it wasn't fleas that kept me from sleeping. During the night, I suffered severe stomach cramps. I blamed the stewed camas — though it could have been the dried salmon. Sandy had eaten more of both than I did, but he was fine. The next day, the pains were worse. I couldn't face another meal. All I wanted was to get back to the fort.

"But you've still to show me where that lupine grows," Sandy protested.

"T'Catisa knows." My words trailed off in a groan.

"Why don't you ask her if she has any medicine that could help you?" Sandy suggested. "She cured your knee last time."

"She can't do anything for this," I said, moaning again.

Chief Cockqua must have agreed. A year ago he'd insisted that T'Catisa use her skill to make me well, but now he seemed to be so eager for us to leave that he offered to send his nephew Kahphoo along to take my paddle.

We set off at first light the next morning. T'Catisa stood on the riverbank, with raindrops glistening on her long black hair. She looked beautiful — and older than when I first saw her. Even in my weakened condition, I noticed that her farewells were directed at Sandy and not at me.

I spent most of the trip back to Fort Vancouver lying in the bottom of the boat, doubled over in pain. Poor Sandy had a hard time matching Kahphoo's steady rhythm. The young Indian was a tireless oarsman and could have paddled all day without a break, but I got him to stop every now and then so that I could make a basin of tea. The tea revived me a little and gave Sandy time to rest.

Once we were back at the fort, I recovered quickly, whereas Sandy moped for days. He showed no interest in the books I lent him, though he cheered up when I suggested that we should help one another learn Chinook. This time his low spirits weren't due to homesickness.

Our lessons went well, and the winter passed quickly. When March came around and it was time for me to leave on the Hudson's Bay Express, Sandy asked me to try and find his brothers, but he showed no interest in going with me. Not that that was a possibility. It was going to be a very strenuous journey. And Sandy was bound to the Company for at least three more years.

*Paeonia brownii* (Brown's peony)

# *My Passenger on the Hudson's Bay Express*

## by Edward Ermatinger
### Fur Trader, Hudson's Bay Company

*Only eighteen papers had suffered, amongst which I
am exceedingly sorry to say is* Paeonia. *This [was]
one of the finest plants in the collection. It often
happens that the best goes first.*

David Douglas' Journal,
May 22, 1827

*Mr. McD's rifle snapped and while he was
endeavouring to distinguish his object in the dark
of the night to have another shot the animal rushed
toward him with the utmost impetuosity. . . . The first
blow the animal gave him he tossed him with great
violence and gored the most fleshy part of the thigh
nearly to the bone.*

Edward Ermatinger's Journal
June 2, 1827

# CHAPTER 14

*The Overland Express*
*March to April 1827*

When Doctor McLoughlin told me that I was to lead the 1827 Hudson's Bay Company Express, he said that several people — Alexander McLeod and himself included — would be joining us for the early part of the journey. He wanted to check on the quality of the skins that were being brought in to Fort Colville, an outpost on the upper Columbia.

The Express traveled across the continent and back once a year — a three-month journey each way — along a route that scaled snowbound mountain passes and followed the meanderings of rivers. The weather was always the unknown factor. So I was stunned when Doctor McLoughlin added, as if it were of no great consequence, "David Douglas will be on the Express as a passenger. He'll be with you all the way to York Factory."

"Mister Douglas, the plant collector?" I asked.

"Yes, the botanist!"

"He'll be the first man who's not an Indian or a *voyageur* to travel the whole northern route." I tried to keep my voice flat and unemotional.

"He has more than proved himself," McLoughlin snapped.

"Of course, sir!"

The Hudson's Bay Company was like the army. One didn't question the orders of a superior. But that didn't mean that I was happy about being saddled with Douglas! This was my first time to lead the Express, and I didn't warm to the idea of being responsible for a plant collector.

The word "passenger" made it sound as if Douglas was going to be carried along in some sort of conveyance, but that wasn't how it was. A passenger had to be prepared to walk long distances at the same pace as the rest of us. He needed to be able to handle a canoe on untamed rivers. And he had to carry his own gear. Any passenger would be a problem, but David Douglas was an unknown quantity.

The man was a conundrum. He didn't look tough, but if the tales they told about him were true, he had great powers of endurance. His eyes bothered him, yet he was a good marksman. He was sometimes withdrawn and moody, but he was well liked. Everyone from Doctor McLoughlin down to young Sandy Ross had good words to say about him.

And there was his passion for flowers and trees! That could cause trouble. If Douglas thought there was a new plant within miles, he had to have it, even at the risk of life and limb. McLeod still talked about the way Douglas had gone out on his own and faced down eight angry Umpquas for the sake of a pine cone.

On the Express, everyone had to work well together. My group consisted of four *voyageurs* and three Iroquois Indians, all men that I knew and trusted. Our job was to deliver the "paper trunk" to York Factory on Hudson Bay—a box that contained mail, accounts, and dispatches. We would travel as far as we could by canoe, and then there would be a long, difficult stretch on foot until we reached Jasper House on the east side of the Rocky Mountains. The trunk was heavy. It weighed over seventy pounds. Three men had to take turns carrying it on their backs along with their own provisions and private baggage. The rest of the gear—tents and supplies—was divided among the other four men.

Douglas would have to carry his own load. In his case, that meant all his collecting material. I'd seen how much he took along on relatively short excursions. This time it would be everything he was taking back to England. I just hoped he realized what lay ahead of him.

With all the extra people and canoes, the journey started out more like a family outing than a serious expedition. The route to Fort Colville was familiar and not overly taxing. Most of the time, David Douglas traveled with Doctor McLoughlin. I didn't see much of him until we reached the fort, which was the end of the line for the Chief Factor. It was also the end of the line for a pair of grouse Douglas had been carrying in his pack for more than two weeks. They were in an oilcloth sack that he tied to his tent pole with a leather thong the first night at Fort Colville. An Indian's dogs came along and ate the birds.

"To think they ended up as a dog's dinner, after I'd carried the cock bird for four hundred and fifty-seven miles and the hen for three hundred and four miles!" he grumbled.

If he was looking for sympathy, he didn't get it. I just pointed out that his load would be that much lighter.

Our first real test came soon after we left Fort Colville. We'd paddled and poled the canoe up the Columbia River and through the Arrow Lakes, where rugged, snowcapped peaks towered over us. Beyond the lakes, the wild river often seemed to lose itself in the mountains. Late one afternoon, we rounded a bend and were faced with a narrow gorge with sides so steep that they shut out the sun. The river tumbled over huge boulders and spilled into dark whirlpools. I ordered two of the Indians to stay in the boat so they could use poles to guide it. The rest of us would make our way along a narrow shelf, hauling on lines attached to the boat.

"Leave your pack in the canoe," I told Douglas.

"It has my seeds and plants in it," he answered, hoisting it onto his back. "I'd sooner carry it in case the canoe doesn't make it."

I refrained from pointing out that if the canoe was lost, none of us would make it. I watched with rising irritation as he adjusted his load. But once we started, he moved as surefooted as a mountain goat along the ledge, and I have to admit that he pulled his weight. When we reached the end of the gorge and looked back down over the way we'd come, we let out a great cheer. We had conquered the impossible!

The next day we faced another obstacle, Dalles des Morts — Death Rapids. The name says it all. This was the most dangerous part of the river. When we came through unscathed, I breathed a little easier. We were going to be a good team. I rewarded the men with an early night.

Douglas and I sat by the fire bringing our journals up to date.

"What did you write about the trip up the rapids?" I asked.

Douglas grinned, then read in a deadpan voice:

*Nothing in the way of plants today!*

"Is that all you had to say?" I asked, shaking my head. That man would rise up and check the flowers on his own grave!

"What about you?" he asked.

I cleared my throat and read:

*Wednesday, 25th. – Thick fog in the morning – fine day. Start at 1/4 past 5 a.m. Course of the river very rapid. Take breakfast at the foot of the Rapid below the Dalles des Morts. Carry all our baggage at the lower brink of the Dalles – haul up our boat safe, tho' it is rather a dangerous place – clear the Dalles about noon.*

After that we got into the habit of comparing journal entries in the evening. Earlier, I had mostly noted the weather, the time we struck camp in the morning, and the distance we traveled. But now that we were reading our entries aloud, I felt I had to add a little more color.

We were drawing close to an important milestone on the trip – the Boat Encampment. It was where we cached the canoe so that I could pick it up in the autumn on the return journey with the westbound Express. After we left the Encampment, we'd be traveling on foot with all our gear on our backs, until we reached Jasper House on the east side of the Continental Divide. That would be our biggest test.

That evening I mentioned to Douglas that my journal entry for the day concerned a plant. The poor man was dismayed that something of botanical interest had escaped his eye – until he found that I'd written about potatoes!

I read the entry aloud:

*Owing to the liberality of the gentlemen by whose posts we passed along the communication [way] we were enabled nearly every night since we left Fort Vancouver to treat ourselves with potatoes at supper and finished the remains of our stock from Fort Colville to-day, probably the first ever eaten at this place.*

"I'm sorry to hear that's the last of the potatoes," Douglas said. "My only botanical reference today is to my seed box." He admitted that he had wandered a bit from the day's main events, but he thought that people back in England might want to know what he carried in his pack. He cleared his throat and began to read:

*Examined the seeds in my tin-box and found them in good order; repacked them without delay and at the same time tied up all my wardrobe, toilet, &c., which is as follows: four shirts (two linen and two flannel), three handkerchiefs, two pair stockings, a drab cloth jacket, vest and trousers of the same, one pair tartan trousers, vest and coat; bedding, one blanket; seven pairs of deer-skin shoes, or as they are called, moccasins; one razor, soap-box, brush, strop, and one towel, with half a cake of Windsor soap. In addition to these I was presented with a pair of leggings by Mr. Ermatinger, made out of the sleeves of an old blanket-coat. . . .*

"Those old leggings hardly deserve a place in your journal!" I protested.

Douglas just smiled and added another line to the day's entry, reading it out loud as he wrote:

*This, trifling as it may appear, I esteem in my present circumstances as very valuable.*

The next morning, we faced a fresh challenge—the Athabasca Pass through the Rockies.

"We'd better divide your load among the rest of us," I said to Douglas while we were eating breakfast. Even though he had more than proven himself, I still worried about the next leg of the journey. Douglas had less experience on snowshoes that the rest of us. If he slowed the pace too much, we'd run out of food before we reached Jasper House.

Of course, he refused the offer. We finally reached a compromise. He let one of the Indians carry his blanket and extra clothing, but he insisted on carrying the tin box that held his journals and precious seeds. It weighed forty-three pounds.

We set off at a steady pace, trudging through deep snow. The crust wasn't strong enough to support us, so we had to put on snowshoes—round *pas d'ours,* or bear paws. We'd bartered with some Indians back along the trail, giving them ammunition and dried salmon in exchange for the shoes. But they turned out to be poorly made. The knots kept slipping and the lacings broke. We'd have done better bringing bigger shoes from Fort Colville—even if it had meant carrying extra weight for a longer distance.

I was glad that Douglas had parted with at least some of his load. He had a hard time getting used to the snowshoes. He kept falling head over heels, or he would sink deep with one leg and stumble over the other. Then he got tangled in the brush with his shoes backside foremost. But he didn't give up! And he didn't complain. The only thing I ever heard him grumble about was that the sun shining on the snow was hard on his eyes.

Our group made a strange picture, climbing up the endless pass, but there was no one to witness it. Nine men strung out across the snowy landscape, each carrying a huge load, one falling and another helping him up, a third lagging far behind, a fourth taking a break while he smoked his pipe, and so on to the end of the line. The course wound steeply uphill, following the wide gravel basin of the Wood River. In the space of ten miles, we forded the river thirteen times, waist-deep in water. Each time we were chilled to the bone. In some places, we had to hang onto one another and cross the river at an angle to fight the current.

"Drag your feet," I reminded the men, as we stepped into the ice-cold water. "Keep them on the bottom. If water gets under your soles, it'll lift you up, and you'll be swept away."

Most mornings we broke camp early—around three o'clock—to take advantage of the crust on top of the snow. During the night, the temperature dropped to a few degrees above zero, but by noon the snow was soft. On top of the physical hardship was the gnawing fear that we might lose our way in the white wilderness. It had been an exceptionally long, hard winter, and the snowpack was so deep that it covered the blaze marks on the trees that showed the route. We couldn't afford the time to do any backtracking. We had to reach the top of the pass before our food ran out, or we would starve.

One morning I had the good luck to bring down a small grouse to add to our meager supplies.

"It's a new species!" Douglas said, examining it. "We can't eat that!"

"You're telling me that you'd have us all starve for the sake of a bird that doesn't exist as far as the rest of the world is concerned!"

"It's my job ... to bring back new species," he said stubbornly.

Maybe I was going slightly crazy, but I handed over the bird!

# CHAPTER 15

*The Hudson's Bay Express*
*May to July 1827*

We reached the top of the Athabasca Pass on the first of May. On the east side of the Rockies, there was less snow and we abandoned the snowshoes. It was a big moment when we all hung our *pas d'ours* on a tree and walked away from them without looking back. Our loads felt pounds lighter.

Two more long days brought us to Jasper House—three small hovels on a bank of the Athabasca River. It was the sort of place where most travelers wouldn't accept a free night's lodging, but after coming over the pass it looked like a luxury hotel to us. Jack Finlay, the musician in our group, discovered an old discarded violin. I brought out my flute, and we made the rafters ring. Soon all us—even David Douglas—were kicking up our heels. After we'd sung ourselves hoarse, the other men called it a day, but Douglas and I sat up awhile talking.

"How did you end up as a Hudson's Bay clerk?" he asked me. "With your music and your interest in books and plays, I'd have thought you'd be happier in a more civilized place."

"I think that myself sometimes," I confessed. "Joining the Hudson's Bay Company was my father's doing. He signed me on along with my brother Francis nine years ago. Francis was nineteen, and I was twenty."

"Where did you grow up?"

"We're from all over. My father was born in Canada, but he moved back to England as a young man and joined the army. He met my mother in Italy. I was born in Elba, and Francis was born in Lisbon. When Mother died, Father sent us to a boarding school in London. If you think life is uncivilized here, you never went to an English boarding school!"

"You're right about that," Douglas agreed. "I never had much schooling at all, though that was mostly my own fault. My father put a high premium on our education. The fact that he could read and write had given him an edge over the other stonemasons. For one thing, he got to carve the names on the tombstones in Scone churchyard! "

I chuckled and then asked, "Where did you learn your botany?"

"I learned a lot about plants from William Beattie, the head gardener at Scone Palace. I was apprenticed to him at the age of eleven. Later, Professor Hooker at Glasgow University let me sit in on his lectures."

"Is your family still in Scone?"

"Only my parents and two of my sisters. My other sister's married. John's apprenticed to an architect, and George is a cashier in a pottery works in Staffordshire."

"It must have taken a bit of courage to strike out on your own the way you have," I said. It seemed a big step from planting flowers at someone else's bidding to roaming the world on his own in search of them.

"Looking for plants was all I ever wanted to do," Douglas answered. "It's what got me expelled from the Dame School when I was three years old! I had to be outside looking at nature. And it was the same when I was older. I could never get to school on time because I had plants to gather or birds to feed. I remember finding a nest of owlets once. I took them home and fed them mice, but when they got bigger I had a hard time catching enough to keep them going. So I spent my lunch pennies on liver from the butcher."

"I never was that set on any one thing," I confessed. I stared into the fire. My dreams were modest. I'd like to settle in a small town somewhere and raise a family. Maybe run a business. And I'd like to write. But even realizing that modest dream would take courage. My father would never understand, and I wasn't sure I would have the nerve to face Doctor McLoughlin and tell him I was quitting the Company.

I wasn't driven like David Douglas.

But some of his determination rubbed off on me on that trip over the Divide. A year later, I left the Company even though they told me that my prospects there were good. I settled in St. Thomas on Lake Erie, where I married the sister of the rector of St. Thomas' Church. All of which has nothing to do with the 1827 Overland Express, except that being in Douglas' company made me think about going after what I really wanted.

Now that we had crossed the Divide, the rivers were once again our highways and we were no longer alone on the trail. We kept running into Indians and fur brigades. Douglas had the same question for everyone. "Have you ever met up with John or Angus Ross from the Orkney Islands? They signed up with the Company about five years ago." He had apparently given his word to Sandy Ross that he'd find the boy's brothers.

Mostly, his questions led nowhere, but every now and then he would meet someone who had a story about brothers from the Orkneys. Most of the stories had a dark ending—an encounter with a grizzly or a drowning. One old trapper remembered meeting a lad named John who had gone to live with the Indians. "Though it may not be your John," he conceded. "It's a common enough name." Another trapper was sure that the young men had quit the Company and returned to the Orkneys to be with a younger brother when they learned their father had drowned.

That was the story that Douglas wanted me to take back to Sandy. He always spoke of the lad fondly. He had helped him with his reading and writing on the way out from England. The boy had a sharp mind, and Douglas thought that in time Doctor McLoughlin could use him as an interpreter. He had picked up the Chinook jargon as fast as he'd picked up reading.

We were all exhilarated by the fast pace of the journey now that we were back on the water—all except Douglas. He would sooner have walked. At the least sign of green, he begged to be put ashore so he could have a closer look at the plants, but I didn't listen. No matter how often Douglas argued that he could keep up with us on foot, I knew he'd soon be left behind.

"That could be a new species of willow," he said, pointing to a nondescript shrub that was just leafing out along the riverbank.

"Leave something for other botanists," I told him. "Maybe Drummond has already named it. He was through here last year when he joined up with Finan McDonald's Express for a while."

"Thomas Drummond, the naturalist with the Franklin Expedition?" Douglas asked.

"The same man!"

This turned out to be the wrong thing to say. It struck a competitive chord in Douglas. Apparently, it wasn't just a question of giving all these new plants names. Douglas had to be the one to do it!

We made such good time that we reached Fort Assiniboine while John Stuart, the Chief Factor, was still gone on a hunting trip around Lesser Slave Lake. When he finally returned, he made up for being late by feeding us caribou steaks and entertaining us with tales of his adventures. After so many weeks together on the trail, we'd all heard one another's stories so often that we knew them by heart, so it was like opening up a new novel to sit around the fire with men from another brigade. Their stories were all about the hardships they had faced — encounters with bears, being frightened by Indians, surviving by eating their moccasins. Stuart had more stories than any of them. He had been a member of Simon Fraser's expedition to the Pacific back in 1808.

"I've survived a lot of storms," he said. "But if you can believe Finan McDonald, I've never seen the conditions the Express endured last year. Even Drummond never saw the like when he traveled in the Arctic."

"McDonald was carrying one of my boxes of seeds," Douglas said. We could tell that his mind was on the fate of his box, not on frostbite and starvation. "He was to take it as far as Fort Edmonton, where I'm to pick it up and carry it from there."

"Drummond would know it was important and make sure it was safe," I reassured him, but that, too, was the wrong thing to say. Douglas didn't trust another botanist to look after his collection.

Now, any worries about Douglas slowing us down were canceled out by his obsession about reaching Fort Edmonton so that he could check on his precious box. There was no holding him back. He insisted on forging ahead on his own. He set off at four o'clock in the morning with a Nipissing Indian guide, who looked to be around seventy years old. The man was reputed to be a good walker. And he'd need to be! Douglas aimed to be at the fort by dark—a forty-three-mile hike over rough country.

When the rest of us reached the fort, traveling at a more leisurely pace, I was relieved to find that Douglas was safe and that his collection had not suffered too much damage. The box was badly dented, but due to Drummond's care, the contents were in better order than Douglas expected. He was sorry to find that one of his favorite plants, a lovely wild peony from the Blue Mountains called *Paeonia brownii*, had not survived.

"It often happens that the best goes first," Douglas said sadly.

After dinner that night, Douglas told me about his adventures on his way to Fort Edmonton. In late May, the land was an endless swamp, saturated from melting snow. He and his guide floundered along, their feet weighed down by mud. Around three in the afternoon, they reached the Sturgeon River. In summer, it was no more than a small muddy stream, but in late spring the banks overflowed.

Douglas figured he'd only have lost three minutes crossing it if he'd been on his own, but his old guide was afraid of the cold water. He got out his small hatchet and spent the next two hours cutting branches and making a raft. This reminded Douglas of his misadventure on the Umpqua, but this time he only needed a small raft. Even so, darkness was creeping in before he and the guide made it across the river.

A few miles farther on, the howling of sled dogs echoed through the air. It was a welcome sound—they were close to the fort.

"See!" the Indian said, pointing to the flickering light of fires.

Douglas looked down in dismay at his mud-caked clothes and boots.

Weary though he was, he retraced his steps to a small lake they'd passed half a mile back, stripped off his clothes, and plunged in. After he'd dried himself and found his linen shirt, he was ready to meet John Rowand, the Chief Factor. An hour later, when he sat down to a fine moose-steak dinner with the gentlemen at the fort, he was glad he'd taken the trouble to make himself presentable. And who should be sitting across from him but Finan McDonald, the leader of the 1826 Express! Douglas was ravenous, not having eaten all day, but first he had to know about his box.

"It was in pretty bad shape by the time it got here," McDonald told him. "But Drummond looked after it. We opened it up together, and he kindly changed all the papers. He said that way the collection would have a better chance of surviving."

After we left Fort Edmonton, we joined up with another brigade. By this time, we were heading down the North Saskatchewan River through the unsafe land of the Stone Indians. We did our best to go unnoticed. I gave the order that there would be no fires after dark. We lashed our boats together in pairs and drifted downstream through the night and the following day, making brief stops morning and evening to cook breakfast and dinner. Needless to say, Douglas found this method of travel very unsuited to collecting; but he did have the chance to find a few plants — milk vetch, phlox, and seven kinds of willow — when we stopped to eat or hunt.

This was buffalo country. Now, when Douglas and I compared journal entries it was more like comparing hunting records. On Thursday, May 31, I wrote:

> *Proceed down the River a few miles till we come up to two of our men who have been absent hunting since yesterday morning. They have each killed a Bull — 16 men set off immediately to bring home the meat — men return with 1 1/2 animals, the rest having been consumed by wolves — continue again a short distance and put ashore where animals appear to be numerous. People go off hunting — return afternoon having killed 11 Bulls — all hands employed carrying the meat to the boats — 1 too lean — thrown away.*

Two days later, Finan McDonald, who had joined us at Fort Edmonton, suffered a horrible accident. It was nearly dark when McDonald, John Harriott, and I closed in on a bull. Harriott fired, but he missed his mark and only wounded the beast. The enraged animal charged McDonald. His rifle misfired, and all he could do was run. He soon realized he wasn't going to reach cover, so he threw himself onto the ground. We could only watch in horror as the bull's first blow tossed him into the air. Everything happened so fast that it was hard afterwards to say how many times the bull attacked McDonald while Harriott and I stood there unable to do a thing. At one point, McDonald cried out, and the bull dropped to the ground as if it had been struck. The animal and the man stayed there, frozen in time, like a painting.

Our boats were about two miles away. Harriott ran off to get help, while I stayed to mark the place. Truly, I had the more difficult task. I couldn't tell if McDonald was still alive, but I didn't dare go closer.

When Harriott returned, we were at a loss as to how to drive the bull away. If we tried to shoot it in the darkness, we might further endanger McDonald — if he wasn't already dead. Suddenly, someone's gun went off by accident. The bull rose, stared in our direction for a moment, and then lumbered off.

We walked slowly toward McDonald, afraid of what we were going to find. Douglas knelt down and listened to his heart. The poor man was in a bad way, but he *was* breathing. His life had been saved by his shot pouch, which was made from a double layer of thick sealskin decorated with porcupine quills and was filled with shot and rags for wadding. It had been gored several times, absorbing blows that would otherwise have pierced McDonald's heart.

Harriott tore some strips from his shirt and handed them to Douglas, who set about binding a huge gash in McDonald's thigh. He eased his pain with opium, giving him twenty-five drops — enough to make sure he would sleep while we carried him to the canoe, which would take him to Fort Carlton, where there was a doctor.

McDonald was lucky — and tough. He lived to tell the tale — again and again! And it grew with each retelling.

The next evening, Douglas admitted to his journal that his desire for seeing such dreadful brutes had cooled.

When we reached Norway House in the middle of June, we felt as if we had returned to civilization. The mail had been brought up from York Factory, reconnecting us with the rest of the world. Douglas' letters contained both good news and bad. There was a letter from Doctor Sabine of the Horticultural Society, telling Douglas that the plants he had shipped on the *William and Ann* had arrived in good condition. Sabine was impressed with Douglas' work. The letter also contained permission for Douglas to cross the continent with the Express! We laughed over the idea that if the answer had been "no," he would have been obliged to walk all the way back!

Douglas' second letter was from his brother John. It brought the sad news of their father's death. Although he had passed away several months earlier, reading it like that in a letter made it seem as if it had just happened. The unexpectedness of the news troubled Douglas. He felt as if he should have known, somehow.

Norway House was where I parted from Douglas. I had to escort the Express to York Factory. But Douglas wouldn't be catching a ship for England until mid-September, so he was in no rush to get to the port. He decided to stay at Norway House for a while and overhaul his collection. He also talked of making a collecting trip farther south to the Red River Valley.

Douglas had one final adventure before he sailed for England. It happened in September after I'd left with the westbound Express, but news of the near-tragedy eventually reached us in Fort Vancouver. Douglas and a few acquaintances rowed out to visit their ship while it was anchored in Hudson Bay. A tremendous storm blew up, and they were unable to return to shore. They were carried some seventy miles out to sea, well out of sight of land. They had to use their hats to bail the water that was washing over the sides of the rowboat. They were given up for lost, but after two days and nights, with the help of the tide, they managed to row back to shore. I'm sure that Douglas' stubborn will must have carried the rest of his companions through the ordeal.

*Olsynium douglasii* (grass widows)

# The End of the Trail

## by Joseph Hooker
### Director of Kew Gardens

*I trust we may yet have a fine jaunt in the Highlands together, perhaps in the summer of 1835.*

> letter from David Douglas to
> Professor Hooker's elder son, William
> October 24, 1832

*Dear Sir: Our hearts almost fail us when we undertake to perform the melancholy duty which devolves upon us, to communicate the painful intelligence of the death of our friend Mr. Douglas, and such particulars as we have been able to gather respecting this distressing providence.*

> letter from Joseph Goodrich and
> John Diell to the British Consul in the
> Sandwich Islands
> Hilo, Hawaii, July 15, 1834

# CHAPTER 16

*London 1870*

As director of Kew Gardens in London, I was in the habit of taking an early morning stroll. That way I could have the gardens to myself. By afternoon, they were usually overrun by pleasure-seekers, even though Kew wasn't designed to be a public park. It was meant for science and for study. Mornings were reserved for botany students and artists. The general public was admitted between one o'clock and six o'clock on weekday afternoons from May through September. The board never stopped arguing about the opening hours, but I saw no need to extend them.

So I was particularly vexed, one summer morning, to find a man sprawled under a tree in the Pinetum. He was obviously neither a student nor a painter. He appeared to be about sixty years old and had a slightly unshaven look. He was dressed in a rumpled tweed suit, but it was his shoes that caught my eye. They were of the moccasin type worn by North American Indians. I couldn't imagine what he was doing in the garden at that early hour.

"Good morning," I said coldly.

"Morning, sir," the man answered, scrambling to his feet.

"May I inquire what you're doing here and how you got in?"

"I walked in last night before the gate closed. When I saw this little pine grove, I didn't fancy going back to my noisy hotel, so I lay down under the trees and went to sleep—the way I've done a hundred times back home."

"And where might home be?" I asked.

I didn't really want to know where he lived. I was just playing for time, hoping to get help in expelling the man from the gardens.

"Home is Oregon," he answered. "But now I'm on my way up to the Orkney Islands. I'm hoping to find my brothers. I set out to find them forty-six years ago when I signed on with the Hudson's Bay Company, but circumstances got in the way."

"That doesn't explain what you're doing in Kew Gardens," I said rather abruptly.

"I came here hoping to get news of David Douglas. I figured they might not know about him in Orkney. It's a fine place, the Orkneys—the way the light reflects back from the water in the lochs and the color of the heather on the hills—but they don't grow trees up there. Mister Douglas was a great tree man. I still remember him going to the Umpqua Valley in search of the sugar pine. T'Catisa said that the tree was his guardian spirit. Otherwise he'd never have gotten back alive with those big cones."

I stared at the man. It had to be our David Douglas he was talking about!

"Seems like people here would know about him because of his interest in plants," he continued, looking at me hopefully.

"I'm sorry . . . so sorry," I stammered. Then I blurted out, "David Douglas is dead. He died . . . a long time ago."

The poor man looked like the wind had been knocked right out of him.

"It was in July 1834. I thought you'd have heard about his sad death in Oregon. . . ." I trailed off. I was wondering how Douglas—alive or dead—could matter so much to an old man who hadn't seen him for over forty years.

"I suppose they knew at the fort, but I left in 1830 as soon as I had my five years in with the Company," the man explained. "That was the year of the big epidemic, when so many people died. Indians and whites. T'Catisa and I moved out to Tillamook on the coast. It was an out-of-the-way place, and we never did get much news after that. Though T'Catisa always said that he was gone."

"T'Catisa?" I repeated, trying to get my thoughts in order. The tragic circumstances of Douglas' death had always troubled me, and I know that my father mourned him to the end of his days.

"T'Catisa was my wife, the mother of our six children. She died last year. I sadly miss her."

"Look! Why don't you come back to my house?" I suggested. "It's right next to the gardens. There's a letter among my father's papers. You should read it. It tells what happened."

As we walked through the gardens, I found myself pointing out plants that Douglas had brought back to Britain, even while I was trying to steer the conversation away from him. Going past the rhododendron beds, I bragged a little about the species that I'd brought back from my own travels in India. Thinking back to that glorious adventure always made me impatient with the petty details that occupied most of my time these days. Disputes over the height of the boundary wall and where to put a new gate. And the never-ending argument about extending the opening hours.

There were some who faulted David Douglas for being restless and dissatisfied after he returned from North America, but I understood how it must have been. At first, he enjoyed being the center of attention, but soon the excitement of being a hero wore off. He didn't want to attend meetings or sit around rewriting his journal. He wanted to be off looking for new plants. I'm sure he wouldn't have turned down the chance for that second expedition, even if he had known how it would end.

We had reached the gate that led from Kew to the private garden behind my house. As I opened it, I said, "We never did introduce ourselves. I'm Joseph Hooker, the director of Kew Gardens."

"Alexander Ross. Though most people call me Sandy."

I led Ross upstairs to my private study, saying, "You must be hungry. I'll have someone bring up breakfast."

"A cup of tea would be nice," Ross answered. "David Douglas always said that tea was the monarch of all food. After some of his most exhausting travels, a basin of tea was all it took to revive him."

While Ross was eating, I searched through my father's papers for a copy of the letter that had brought word of Douglas' sad end. I let Ross finish his breakfast before handing it to him.

Ross passed it back, saying, "I'd sooner you read it to me."
I flushed with embarrassment.

The old man must not know how to read. Stumbling over my words, I explained that the letter telling about the accident had been sent to my father, Professor William Hooker. It was written by two missionaries who lived in Hilo, Hawaii. I cleared my throat and began to read.

*Dear Sir: Our hearts almost fail us when we undertake to perform the melancholy duty which devolves upon us, to communicate the painful intelligence of the death or our friend Mr. Douglas, and such particulars as we have been able to gather respecting this distressing providence.*

The letter continued with a long, tangled introduction. Before I was halfway through it, Ross interrupted me. "So what happened to him?"

I abandoned the letter.

"He fell into a pit that had been dug for trapping bulls," I told him. "He was trampled to death by a bull that had fallen in earlier. He was on his way to meet up with these two missionaries. He'd promised to take them to see a volcano."

"The trail that fell away in front of him," Ross said softly.

"There are questions about his death that have never been answered," I continued. "Douglas had been warned about the pits. There were three of these bull pits near a watering hole — two along the trail and one off to the side. Ned Gurney told him to watch out for them. They were covered over with brush."

"Douglas had trouble with his eyes," Ross said.

"But the pit should have been obvious," I argued. "After all, a bull had already fallen into it and would have broken the brush cover. Some people think David Douglas was murdered and his body was tossed into the pit. And they have a suspect in Ned Gurney. He was an ex-convict from Botany Bay."

"Did Douglas have a little dog with him?" Ross asked.

The question took me by surprise.

"There was a dog," I answered. "His Scotch terrier, Billy. He was sitting by the trail guarding Douglas' pack when the men discovered the body. But what made you think there might be a dog?"

Ross didn't answer the question.

"Douglas wasn't murdered," he said firmly. "It was an accident. He was alone when it happened — except for the little dog."

"What makes you say that?"

"T'Catisa saw it. She saw Douglas with his little dog in her dreams . . . walking down a trail that suddenly fell away. She always called him Olla-piska. When she stopped dreaming about him, she knew that Olla-piska had reached the end of his trail. I didn't come here expecting to find him — though it is still a bit of a shock to know he's gone. I only wanted to make sure he hadn't been forgotten."

I'm a scientist. I deal with facts. I don't put much faith in dreams. Yet, I found myself taking comfort from the way Ross was so sure that David Douglas' death had been a tragic accident. Douglas had been such a gentle, trusting man that I couldn't bear the thought of someone murdering him.

"You don't need to worry about him being forgotten," I told Ross. "Not with his name attached to so many plants — *Aster douglasii, Gentiana douglasii, Iris douglasiana, Lotus douglasii, Viola douglasii.* I could go on and on! And, of course, there's the Douglas fir. He brought back the seeds. There's a tree in Scone Palace gardens from a seed he sent home in '25. It's already a good size."

But Ross wasn't listening.

"I always said he never should have killed that albatross!" he burst out.

"The albatross?" I repeated.

"He killed it when we were sailing down the coast of South America. When I said we'd all pay for his folly, he answered that if anyone paid, it would be him — that he wouldn't be the first collector to fail to reach home with his treasures. He just hoped he'd be rewarded with some small measure of success."

"Every garden in Britain owes a debt to David Douglas," I assured him.

"I owe him a great debt myself," Ross said. "He taught me how to read."

"I thought you didn't know how . . . when you didn't take the letter."

"I can read well enough," Ross answered. "It was just that I couldn't make out that small, cramped handwriting! My eyes aren't as good as they were."

"I didn't know David Douglas was ever a teacher," I said, looking puzzled. "When was that?"

Ross launched into the wildly improbable story about how he'd learned to read on the *William and Ann* on his way to the Pacific Northwest. He'd signed up to serve the Hudson's Bay Company as some sort of clerk when the only thing he could read or write was his own name. Douglas had told him he was lucky to be called Alexander Ross because he shared so many letters with the word *albatross*. That was the first word Ross ever read, and his primers had been Douglas' books on birds and flowers.

"Though there were times that first summer at the fort, when I wished I'd never learned," Ross continued. "I told myself that if I hadn't been able to read, Doctor McLoughlin would have sent me right back home when the *William and Ann* left in September. That's what I wanted. I was so homesick for the Orkney Islands that I could hardly stand it out there. I suppose I was lonely, being that much younger than everyone else."

"You must have gotten over it," I said.

"Whenever David Douglas showed up at the fort, I got to feeling better again. His passion for flowers was catching. I began to look for them, too. And he got me interested in learning the Chinook jargon. In December 1826, a few months before he left to cross the continent, he took me on a trip to the coast to meet his friend Chief Cockqua. Douglas wanted me to know the area, so that I could go back again the following year and collect some lupine seeds for him. I was fifteen, and Cockqua had a beautiful daughter named T'Catisa. The next summer, she showed me the meadow where the *tlopit* grows. I can still see her standing there with the white petals sprinkled on her black hair like confetti. . . ."

Ross ran out of words. The memory seemed to be too much for him.

Sandy Ross and I traded tales about Douglas for the next hour or two. By then, the manner of Douglas' death didn't seem quite so important, though at one point I said something about how his failing eyesight must have made his future look bleak. Douglas wouldn't have had much of a life if he hadn't been able to identify his beloved plants.

"That's not for us to judge," Ross answered sharply. "Olla-piska was a man with fire in his soul. It takes courage to rise above poverty and a lack of schooling the way he did. I've no doubt that he'd have met blindness with courage, too."

When Ross got up to leave, I asked him to come again so that we could talk some more.

He shook his head. "Thanks! But I got what I came for. Maybe someday, when I go back to Oregon to see my children, I'll take the name Douglas fir with me. There, we mostly call it the Oregon pine, but I think Douglas fir is more fitting."

After Ross left, I leafed through my father's papers until I found another letter. It was addressed to my older brother, William. I read it aloud, wishing I'd shared it with Ross:

*You may tell your little brother (who wondered that I could bear to go to sea, as there were cockroaches in all ships) that I now feel a mortal antipathy, even more than he, if possible, to these insects; for having made a great number of observations in the Sandwich Islands, the vile cockroaches ate up all the paper, and as there was a little oil on my shoes, very nearly demolished them too!*

I was the "little brother" who didn't like cockroaches. I never did get over my dislike of them, and I saw more than my share of them in India. My eyes misted over as I read the lines:

*I trust we may yet have a fine jaunt in the Highlands together, perhaps in the summer of 1835.*

It was not to be.

After I'd put the letter away, I sat for a while longer, my thoughts drifting from Douglas to Kew Gardens and back again. I decided to propose to the board that they enlarge the Pinetum. The south side of the lake would be a good location. And those rather forlorn deodar cedars could be replaced with Douglas firs. The cedars hadn't thrived, but Douglas firs would.

I attended another endless meeting that afternoon. I

reluctantly agreed to the use of carpet bedding along the edges of the paths, though I saw no need for a blaze of gaudy color. I like a more natural look. Of course, the matter of opening hours was raised once again. This time, I held my tongue.

That evening, standing in the gardens with the sun going down over the lake, I pictured how the Pinetum would look a hundred years from now. You don't plant a garden just for today. You plant it for the future. I thought I would group species from the Old World and New World genera facing each other. And people would keep on coming — all of them with their own aims and needs. There was really no way to recognize a serious student. I had just realized that if my father hadn't welcomed a certain young undergardener with very little formal education to his botany lectures in Glasgow fifty years ago, Kew Gardens wouldn't be what it is today.

# AUTHOR'S NOTE

David Douglas was born in the village of Scone in Scotland on June 25, 1799. He began his career as an apprentice gardener at the age of eleven. By the time he was in his mid-twenties, he was a respected botanist and explorer. In 1824, the Royal Horticultural Society sent Douglas to the west coast of North America, where he spent two years in what is now Oregon, searching for seeds of plants that could be grown in English gardens. Among the hundreds of species of plants that Douglas collected were the cones of the Douglas fir—the tree that now bears his name.

Looking for plants does not sound nearly as exciting or as demanding as tracking wild animals in the forest. After all, plants stay in one place, waiting to be found. But as I read David Douglas' journal, I discovered a man of great courage and determination —especially determination.

David Douglas was passionate about plant hunting. By his own estimate, he covered over seven thousand miles in the Pacific Northwest, traveling on foot and by canoe. He was not particularly robust, but he often walked for weeks on end through the roadless wilderness, getting by with very little food. He had poor eyesight, but he could bring down a pine cone from a two-hundred-foot-tall tree with a single rifle shot. He was a solitary man, but he got along with people from many different backgrounds, from professors to fur trappers to Indians. The Indians named him Olla-piska, which means "fire" in the Chinook jargon.

In writing *Olla-piska*, I relied on other journals in addition to that of David Douglas. John Scouler, the ship's doctor on the *William and Ann*, kept a record of his travels. So did Edward Ermatinger, the leader of the Hudson's Bay Company Express. Incidents throughout the story—such as meeting William Clark on Robinson Crusoe's island, Chief Futillifum's sudden death, and the buffalo misadventure—all come from the journals.

Sandy Ross (not to be confused with trapper Alexander Ross, who came west with the Pacific Fur Company in 1811) is my own invention. On a visit to the Orkney Islands several years ago, I was fascinated to learn that Hudson's Bay Company ships used to stop at Stromness to take on recruits. It must have been a shock for youths who had grown up on a treeless island to find themselves in the old-growth forests of North America! I filed that away as a story idea. It resurfaced in my mind when I needed a cabin boy on the *William and Ann*. Cabin boys do not keep journals, so I had to make up his background.

T'Catisa, the only other character who is fictional, is based on a young girl who is mentioned several times in Douglas' journal. She was the daughter of Chief Cockqua and wove the three hats that the Indian chief traveled a long distance to present to Douglas. She also collected huckleberry seeds for him.

In one of the many earlier drafts of this book, Sandy Ross was Douglas' helper and the narrator of the entire story. But that did not capture the essence of Douglas' adventures, since he spent most of his time traveling alone or with an Indian guide. In the end, I chose to have several different narrators, which gave me more scope in telling Olla-piska's story. It let me look back on his contribution to botany through the eyes of Joseph Hooker, the director of Kew Gardens in London, who was the son of Douglas' friend and mentor, Sir William Hooker, a botany professor at Glasgow University.